RIDES A STRANGER

**Center Point
Large Print**

**This Large Print Book carries the
Seal of Approval of N.A.V.H.**

RIDES A STRANGER

BILL BROOKS

CENTER POINT PUBLISHING
THORNDIKE, MAINE

This Center Point Large Print edition
is published in the year 2009 by
arrangement with Golden West Literary Agency

Copyright © 2007 by Bill Brooks

The text of this Large Print edition is unabridged.
In other aspects, this book may vary
from the original edition.
Printed in the United States of America.
Set in 16-point Times New Roman type.

ISBN: 978-1-60285-441-3

Library of Congress Cataloging-in-Publication Data

Brooks, Bill, 1943–
  Rides a stranger : the journey of Jim Glass / Bill Brooks.
    p. cm.
  ISBN 978-1-60285-441-3 (library binding : alk. paper)
  1. Large type books. I. Title.
  PS3552.R65863R53 2009
  813′.54—dc22
2008053281

For Carmen and Laura,
God's Own Children

PROLOGUE

The Hondo Daily Reporter
Eyewitness Account of Slaying

My name's Kip Mulligan and I own a saloon in Hondo County just outside Mordecai, New Mexico Territory. I have owned the place for three years and never seen such violence all at once. About noon, three men came into my establishment and took seats at a table and ordered drink and food. They were secretive in their manner and spoke in low voices. I took them at first to be cowboys, for they were dressed like drovers and wore long dusters and spurs with small rowels.

I brought them whiskey and stew and they took to it like they had not eaten in quite some time. I tried to make small talk but they were reticent to be engaged in conversation. One of them had his hair in a long braid that fell halfway down his back. That was the only outstanding feature among them.

I noticed that their horses were all lathered when I stepped outside to empty a spittoon. They looked like they had been used pretty hard.

My assistant, Miss Emily Rose Sherbrooke, entered the room shortly after the trio arrived and took up residence with me behind the bar. Some words were exchanged between she and the men not fit for print. I tried to intervene on her behalf after they insulted her, making reference to what they perceived her profession to be. Miss Sherbrooke has worked for me for several years and is an entertainer and nothing more, let the record show.

It was at this point that I became concerned for our safety, for all three of the men acted gruff and in a threatening manner and I could see by then they were well-armed with revolvers. I asked Miss Sherbrooke to take her leave so as to calm the situation. She refused, calling one of them a son of a —! after he again insulted her looks. This is when he parted his duster back and showed us he was wearing a badge—the sort I'd seen whilst living in Texas and quite common down in that country, the sort the Rangers wear.

I offered them a free bottle of spirits in order to improve the situation and they readily accepted, and I thought that pretty much the end of the matter even though Miss Sherbrooke was still distressed over the insults they'd cast her way.

Things had settled down considerably by the time another stranger entered and approached the bar behind which I and Miss Sherbrooke were yet standing and ordered a glass of beer. He took notice of the painting I have hanging above the bar —a rendering of a nude entitled <u>Eros in Recline</u>, which I purchased a year earlier at an auction in Santa Fe in order to provide my customers some respite from the isolation of the territory, which only adds to a man's great loneliness. The painting is quite revealing and free to view for any paying customer.

Nonetheless, the stranger seemed like everyone else who comes in for a drink— nothing at all unusual about him. He was middle-aged, maybe, tall, dusty from the trail like the other three. When he first came in I thought maybe he was part of that bunch because he was wearing a duster of similar fashion.

He kept glancing up at that painting before letting his gaze fall to the mirror behind the bar, and I did not understand what he was doing until he done it.

Cool as a cucumber, he reached inside

his coat, I thought to pay for the beer, but when he withdrew his hand, it was full of a nickel-plated Russian model Smith & Wesson 44.-40, I do believe. I feature myself as something of a gun fancier and have studied the various models of revolvers, and the Russian model is a mean piece of iron, that when you've emptied its firepower on your opponents you can use to bludgeon them with if needed. I've seen it done.

Miss Sherbrooke and I were warned off sounding the alarm by the stranger's hard gaze—not that I would have alerted them anyway considering their earlier behavior toward Miss Sherbrooke.

And as smooth as silk the stranger swung 'round and pointed his piece at the trio and warned them to lay their own pistols on the table they were sitting at. I never saw a man hold a gun so steady, and you'd have to be a complete fool to not think he meant business.

But I guess those three were fools. The one with the braid swore a curse and made his play but by the time he'd cleared leather, the stranger shot him dead center. Dust spanked up off his shirt and he flopped back out of his chair like a carp yanked out of the river.

The sound of that Russian model going off in such close quarters left my ears ringing. Miss Sherbrooke screamed just as the remaining pair went for their guns, coming up quick out of their chairs as they did. I don't know what those boys were thinking—whether they had a death wish or whether maybe just because they were peace officers they knew all about looking into the face of danger and terrible odds and were not fazed by what they just witnessed happen to their friend. I know those Texas Rangers are tough hombres.

The stranger killed them both so quick it sounded like he only fired a single shot. Bang bang.

I never seen anything like it in my life, and I've resided in such places as Dodge City and Tombstone and Del Rio, Texas too.

Then before I could even think to breathe he wheeled about and aimed his weapon at me—the muzzle of that big Russian model breathing smoke an inch from my face, and he said, "Whatever you're thinking about doing, don't."

And I said, "No, sir, I ain't thinking about doing nothing and I ain't going to either." And then he looked at Miss Sherbrooke and said, "Miss, please stop that god—

screaming." It shut her mouth right up like a door that had been slammed shut.

We watched as he walked over to the dead men and removed their badges and put them in his pocket. Then just turned and went out and got on his horse and rode off toward the north. That's how it happened. I don't know how I'm ever going to get those bloodstains out of the floorboards. If any of your readers want to come by and see where those three Texas Rangers got dusted, they can see the exact spot. That's all I've got to say about what I seen.

No, I never seen the man before in my life, nor did I see those three Rangers. It seemed odd to me that they had come to Hondo County from across the border in Texas, and I remember when I first saw their badges that I asked them how it worked, them enforcing the law in New Mexico, and what the one said—the one with the braid of hair—was, "We ain't surveyors." "Surveyors!" I said, taking it to mean they didn't care nothing about where borders began and ended. I don't know what else it could have meant. I reckon now they're sorry they weren't surveyors. My place is open for business all the time.

CHAPTER ONE

After I turned the badges into Captain Rogers in Eagle Pass, he thanked me for what I'd done and said, "Jim, I wish you could have brought those murdering bastards in alive so I could have hanged them myself."

I told him I wished I could have too but they didn't give me much of a chance to negotiate.

"It's one thing to kill one of my men," he said, "another to kill three and steal their badges and guns. To me, it's robbing the dead, which only makes the crime worse, and even though I am sworn to uphold the law, had I been you I don't think I would have negotiated with them either."

Captain Rogers was a short, blue-eyed man who'd spent most of his adult life fighting for the right things. He'd pulled me out a jail cell where I was doing thirty days for drunk and disorderly and bought me a decent meal and said he was sorry to have seen me go downhill like I had done. I said I was sorry too. Then he told me about the killings and said, "You want to be a Ranger again?" I'd most likely have turned him down but I knew all three of those boys—Frank May, Billy Higgens, and Josiah Barkley. Two had wives and children, and I knew them too. And when the Captain told me how they'd been ambushed and then executed by being shot in the back of the head, I could see myself finding the men who did it. And I could see myself doing what I did to their killers—which is exactly what happened that day in Hondo County where I found them.

Then I told the Captain I was quitting for good, I didn't want to wash my hands in any more blood. He asked what I'd do, and I said I thought I'd go work at something peaceful like on a ranch somewhere, and we shook hands and that was the end of my Rangering days and the start of all the rest of my days.

And now I was on the drift again like I had been since I quit.

I'd bet a dollar that the crow watching me from atop the wobbling sign wondered what such a raggedy looking fellow like me was doing riding a twenty dollar horse with a forty dollar saddle into a town that looked like little more than some old lumber somebody had spilled off the back of their wagon and had been hammered up into badly constructed buildings on a prairie so lonesome even the wind never stopped to take a rest.

And I'll bet another dollar I wouldn't have an answer.

The sign read:

COFFIN FLATS POP. 756
NO DISCHARGING OF FIREARMS
BY ORDER OF CITY MARSHAL
WELCOME

Summer was dying and winter hadn't woke up yet. Some called it "Indian summer." All I know was it was a sweet time of year—not too hot, nor cold—and I'd come a long ways from the last place I'd been and was thirsty and tired. I was also down to my last few dollars from the last job I quit, when the ramrod told me to go dig Mr. Watts some postholes, which was the last straw for me, considering what all had preceded it.

I told the ramrod I didn't dig postholes, and he said that I'd better go collect my pay then because he was only paying for a posthole digger that day and not some fancy duded-up cowboy who thought himself too high and mighty to do work except from the back of a horse. I said that was about the size of it. But where he got the idea I was high and mighty escaped me even though I wasn't about to disabuse him of his notions. Hell, I figured I'd already gone the extra mile by mending fence wire, something no man worth his salt should ever do.

So I went on up to the big house where Mr. Watts lived and knocked on the door, and his wife answered and looked surprised to see me. I told her I was quitting. She asked why and I told

15

her my hand didn't fit a posthole digger was why and she rolled her eyes.

"Lord, Jim, it seems like such a little thing to be quitting over."

"It may well be, Fannie, but that's the way it is."

But we both knew it wasn't *just* about me digging postholes or not digging them. It went a lot beyond all that.

Now I guess a stranger listening in might wonder why a saddlesore drover like myself would be talking so familiarly with the rancher owner's wife on such a pretty day as it was, standing there on that big wide wraparound porch so freshly painted you could still smell the mineral spirits. And I'd have a hard time explaining it except to say that Fannie Watts and me had gotten on familiar terms ever since about the second week I'd come to work on the place.

Some things just happen you don't have any control over—like the feeling that comes over you about certain women and horses and other potentially dangerous creatures. That's the way it was with us—we didn't have any control over it.

The way it happened was, I was out riding fence, looking for busted wire I could fix so all Mr. Watts's cattle didn't run clear to Colorado or some such, when this black buggy topped a grassy rise and come on down the fence line.

She pulled up and stopped where I was banding wire back together and set there watching me. I was at first pretending like I hadn't noticed because I knew who she was and what the ramrod had warned me of the first day I hired on.

He'd said, "Jim Glass, don't make the mistake some other of these old waddies have made and gotten run off for."

"What mistake would that be?" I had told him as I threw my bedroll onto an empty bunk in a place you could tell was lived in by nothing but men because there were chaps hanging on pegs and run-down boots 'neath the cots, several decks of dog-eared playing cards, and lariats and everything smelling of sweat and tobacco smoke.

"Flirting with the boss's wife," he'd said with a face like a preacher that just learned there wasn't any Jesus.

"That been a longstanding problem?" I asked, looking around at my new home—for how long, exactly, I didn't know, but knew it wasn't someplace I'd likely retire in.

"No, no problem," he'd said, "long as you keep your eyes to yourself and your manners proper. She's younger than the old man and cute as a button and sometimes these old boys just fall all over themselves whenever she comes around. Some don't rightly know where to draw the line 'cause they was raised without manners."

17

"Maybe it's her that's the problem then," I said. "Maybe she oughtn't to come around men who don't see a decent woman but maybe thrice a year whenever they hit a town where there might be some decent women to be seen."

"You hold your tongue or you can just saddle that broomtail and keep riding," he'd told me. He was a stumpy little fellow hard as weathered blackjack tree who'd left any personality God had given him back home somewhere.

So anyway, I tried to keep everything to myself whenever I saw her—Fannie—and not talk about it with any of the other hands, about what a pert young gal she was, with hair like spun gold, to be somewhat poetical about it, and eyes as crisp blue as a Kansas sky on a real good day. She looked more like the boss's daughter than his wife whenever you saw them together.

Jack Watts was tall and slightly bent forward like a nail that had been struck slightly wrong. And you'd never see him without his standing under a big white Stetson that looked like he'd just taken it off the merchant's shelf. He had flowing white moustaches, and most of what hair he had on his head was *all* white as well and shagged over his collar. He wore black waist-coats and white shirts. Flint, the ramrod, said old Jack Watts started out as a drover back in '68 and eventually gathered his own little herd made up of mostly mavericks and maybe more

than a few brand-altered cattle and started buying up other surrounding ranches, owned by
many who had abandoned life on the high lonesome for the goldfields of California.

"Everything that old boy touches turns to
gold," Flint said. "Like that fella, Midas."

"Including the wife?"

"Yeah, her too, I reckon."

So there she was, sitting in that little black
buggy with the wind blowing down the grass
and letting it back up only to knock it down
again, and even a man laced with sweat and sore
hands could look upon that sea of green and see
it was a damn pretty sight, when the wind waved
through it. Mrs. Watts—Fannie—sat there in that
buggy looking at me with those eyes looked like
the kind painted on the face of a bisque doll,
and she was even prettier than the land.

She said "Hidey," and I said "Hidey" back and
let go of the wire and the wrecking bar and took
off my old Stetson and wiped my sleeve across
my sweated face while I watched her reach
down somewhere under the seat and come up
with a mason jar sweating about as much as I
was and hold it forth.

"Would you like some cold tea?" she said, and
it didn't take me very long at all to answer that
I would. And each of us stood there holding
onto it a moment, looking into each other's
eyes, and you could just feel whatever it was

19

dancing between us like the heat waves you see wobbling off a road in the summer.

Then she asked did I want something to eat, was I hungry?

Of course I was, even if I wasn't, and she reached down into a basket where she'd brought the jar of tea from and I could see other jars in there as well and handed me a sandwich wrapped in butcher paper.

"Hope you like roast beef and onions," she said, handing it to me.

"Love 'em," I said.

Then we stood there looking at each other a good bit longer before she said she had to ride on and deliver some of the other men their lunch, and I said, "Yes'm," because there wasn't any words for what I was feeling and thinking that I could have said other than yes'm.

I watched her drive off and my heart wasn't in any more work that day, or the next, when she didn't return. Instead it was Flint come riding up and pitched me down a jar of tea and a sandwich without those same loving looks.

"I was sort of hoping it would be the boss's wife bringing me lunch," I said. "It sort of breaks up the meanness of this type work."

He looked at me so hard with those dark empty eyes of his it was like looking down the barrels of a shotgun.

"I ain't gon' warn you twice," he said, and

drove off in that rickety buckboard like some sort of king riding in a one man parade.

Next two days it was the same thing, Flint bringing me and the rest of us lunch, and I'd bet another dollar the other boys were just as disappointed as I was and did believe those sandwiches and that tea didn't taste as good as when the boss's wife brought them.

Then come that Friday there she came, up over the rise in that little black buggy pulled by the bay, and I quick sniffed my shirt to see how bad it was I stunk and it was pretty bad considering the weather had been awful hot for days and days, so bad even the wind laid down and didn't blow half the time. You could look off in the distance every now and then and see a windmill that wasn't turning, and the sky was empty of birds flying, and stream water was warm as fever.

I knocked dust out of my hat by slapping it against my leg and set it back on my head and tried to seem casual about it as she pulled up and stopped. This time I didn't try and pretend I hadn't noticed her coming and instead stood there with my hands stuffed down into my hind pockets like I was at some pie dance waiting to be asked to join in a quadrille.

"Hidey, Jim," she said, only this time she said it using my first name.

"Hidey, m'am," I said back, still unsure what little game we were engaged in.

I wasn't completely bereft of the ways of women. In fact I'd known my share of them. But most of them were what you'd call "improper" types—Cyprians, Brides of the Multitudes, Fallen Angels—that sort. Goodhearted girls as long as you had a dollar or two to buy them a drink or afford their services. Sad women, lots of them were, looking for a man richer than a cowboy to take them out of the life and set them up proper. Some made it too, and some drank mercury. But it had been a quite a little time since I'd been in the company of a woman like Fannie Watts, and I guess I was acting like it too.

We stood there staring, not saying much, and it felt a little like ants crawling in my shirt from the trickling sweat and the anticipation so much so I could hardly stand it.

"Been a while," I said.

"Oh, I had to go to visit my mother," she said. "But I'm back now."

"I reckon you got to get on and take the others their lunch," I said, testing the waters because I'd just as soon she was gone as to stand there and have to be around her knowing she was as illegal as that whiskey they sold down in the Indian Nations.

"No," she said, reaching into her little basket and taking out a sandwich and a jar of tea. "I saved you until last today, Jim. Would you give me a hand down? I'd like to stretch my legs."

Well, it just all got better from there on. As we were later lying in the grass together looking up at big white clouds drifting overhead that had no rain in them, I was thinking about the warning Flint had laid on me the first day. But the truth was, I knew that it didn't matter because nothing good ever lasted very long anyway and you learned to take the good where you found it and expect the worst to come along right behind it.

Fact, I told myself Flint and the rest could come and shoot me and string me up and shoot me again, and it would have been worth it the way I was feeling just then. I believe a man can die happy if he tries hard enough, and I sure gave it my all. I think the look on Fannie's face could attest to how much of my all I gave it.

And so we met like that two or three times a week until I had pretty much fallen down in the well of love over her and was planning how many banks I'd need to rob to give Fannie the sort of life she was accustomed to if she ran off with me when the cold hard truth came down like a bad rain.

Truth had a name: Junior Bosch. He was another hand working on Watts's spread. Junior was a good ten years younger than me, and admittedly of a pleasant disposition. On top of which he had dark curly hair and teeth that shone like ivory that caused even some of the old punchers to look upon him with a certain envy.

It seemed I wasn't the only one getting those special delivery lunches from Fannie—that she often alternated days between Junior and me as to which of us got our lunch delivered last. And once all the dirty laundry got washed, I learned there were some days when Junior and me both got our lunches delivered back to back. And that little trip she said she took to her mother's turned out to be a trip to meet up with yet another fellow in Council Bluffs. Most disturbing to me was having to think I was mixing in where Junior might have earlier been.

The real kicker was, I think Flint knew the whole while what sort of woman she was and was laughing out the side of his ugly mouth at those who'd been fool enough to fall for Fannie's charm. He fired Junior when it came to light because Junior had a loose mouth on him when he got to drinking and ran the whole tale down in front of me and the others one night. I didn't get fired because to that point nobody knew about me and Fannie. 'Course, Flint told everybody to keep it under his hat what Junior had spilled, that he didn't want Mr. Watts hearing such things or he'd fire every one of us. But I knew then and there I was gone.

So I made a big show of quitting the next day after I learned about the two of them doing the grass dance together—an image that set with me about like a rancid steak washed down by snakehead whiskey. Flint had come up to me first thing in the morning and told me to go dig some postholes up on the west forty. That's when I told him what I thought about such work—and it was by God the truth even if it wasn't the real reason I quit.

But my pride wouldn't let me come right out and tell Fannie face-to-face what I was thinking, the reason I was quitting. And hers wouldn't let her ask any deeper than the reason I gave her; I think in a way she was glad I was going.

And so there I stood and there she stood and you could tell it was all broke and never going to get fixed between us and the only difference was I think I cared a whole lot more than she did. Out of work cowboys were as plentiful as ticks on a wet dog, and beautiful young women were about as rare as a butcher with all his fingers, so you can see which the odds favored.

So she went and got my thirty dollars a month's pay and handed it to me.

"I'm sorry things didn't work out, Jim," she said, and I could hear the old man inside somewhere coughing and it dawned on me just then he must have known of her dalliances, past and present. How could he have not? And knowing he must have known left me feeling pretty lowdown to think that she done what she done with his knowing it and I'd become equally as guilty.

Still, when I looked into those sweet eyes I couldn't get mad at her.

"You even feel a little bit bad about all this?" I said.

She glanced up at me and said, "Well, it all works out somehow, doesn't it, Jim."

"Goddamn if it don't," was the last words I said to that woman, my heart broken, my mind messed up like it sometimes got when I drank the better stuff.

So I rode on away from there just following the sun because it was as good a direction to go as any, and then here I come to this sign all about no discharging of firearms and population of 756, thinking it wasn't too big of a town where a man would feel crowded, but not so small either that there wouldn't be any job opportunities. I needed some grub and to find work of some sort, or me and my horse would end up just another of life's tragic victims—our bones bleaching on the plains like a lot of others who'd gone in search of something they weren't ever going to find—men, women, and children. Here and there along the roads you could often see little wood markers with names burned into them half knocked over by the wind and rain and I didn't feature joining them as part of that grim landscape.

I never thought my stopping in such a place called Coffin Flats, with such low expectations, would lead to what it did. But then, after my last go-round, I told myself, Jim, don't even try and guess what is writ in the book of life under your name.

I just rode on in and tied off in front of the first drinking establishment I found. Place called Bison Bill's Emporium.

If the beer was cold and wet and not over a dime a glass, it was my sort of place.

CHAPTER TWO

I rested a foot on the rail and waited for Bison Bill or whoever it was tending bar this mid-morning. A one-armed man with handlebar moustaches said, "Beer or whiskey?"

A chalkboard listed the prices. Beer was a nickel, whiskey two bits, pickled eggs a dime.

"Beer," I said, "and two of those pickled eggs."

It was early yet to be drinking, but then, I never owned a watch. There was just me and the one-armed bartender and a man sitting by himself in the corner at a table reading a newspaper —holding it up to the window light because it was dim inside the place.

He lowered his paper when I ordered my beer, looked over the top of the pages at me then went back to reading.

I put two bits on the bar and the one-armed man picked it up and put it in a big brass cash register after he punched a button and the drawer clanged open. I wondered how much money a big register like that could hold; just weighing my options for a future career as desperado in case nothing better came along. I sure didn't want to go mending any more fences, even if the ranch owner's wife was pretty and liberal with her body.

"What time you put out the regular eats?" I said, plopping one of the eggs into my trap before washing it down with a swallow of beer.

"Not till the lunch crowd," he said.

I ate the other egg and sipped more beer and it was cold and that's all that mattered, cold and wet, something to cut the trail dust.

"You in town looking for work?" he said.

I heard the newspaper rattle behind me.

"Could be. You know of any?"

"Not much."

I waited for him to come up with a name maybe. Some towns are just friendlier than others.

"Where you hail from, you don't mind my asking?"

"Bar Double Z," I said. "Nebraska."

"I fell drunk off a horse once in Nebraska," he said.

"I imagine you'd not be the first to do so," I said.

It was aimless talk not leading to anything I could see.

"Noon you say, about the lunch?"

"Yes, that's right."

I glanced at the jar of pickled eggs again.

"You do your own pickling?" I said.

The barkeep smiled.

"I seen you," he said, "I was wondering if maybe you'd come in for the big fight tonight." He was wiping out the inside of a drink glass, then holding it up to the poor light and wiping it some more.

"What fight's that?" I said.

"Gentleman Harry Ford is in town taking on all comers. Champeen prizefighter from back East somewhere. Middleweight they say."

"Middleweight, huh?"

He pointed to a poster tacked up on the wall just inside the door.

"Cost you five dollars to get in, but if you can knock the champ out, his manager will give you fifty dollars."

"Ten to one," I said, scratching up under my hat. I needed a bath and a shave and some clean clothes. "Not too bad of odds."

"No sir. If I had both arms, I'd fight him myself."

"You say all a fellow has to do it knock him out?"

That's when the fellow reading the newspaper

lowered it and said, "You'd be wise to save your money and your face."

I glanced over at him.

He looked like a banker with his derby cocked to one side and frock coat and checked vest. All he was missing was a horse collar and a necktie. He folded his newspaper and set it beside his coffee cup. I could see the window light glance off a pinky ring.

"What makes you think I'd lose?" I said.

He lifted his cup and took a drink, his eyes watching me the whole time like I was a dog he was thinking of buying.

"I know you cow punchers all think you can fight, especially when you're all liquored up. You believe you can whip Jesus himself, but trust me, this old boy will use you like a red-headed stepchild. I saw him fight an exhibition in Dodge last year."

Well, shit, it sure didn't help my confidence none having a stranger tell me he could tell just by the looks of me what I could and could not do in a fistfight.

"Where do I sign up for this Gentleman Harry Ford?" I said to the barkeep, and he smiled like he'd just grown a new arm.

"The fight's to be held down at Bucky's Corral. Starts at seven o'clock sharp. Bring your money."

"Goddamn right," I said, and looked back over my shoulder at the man. He simply picked up his newspaper and tucked it under his arm and walked out into the mid-morning light that seemed to just swallow him whole.

"Who is that fellow?" I said.

"City marshal Chalk Bronson," he said.

"Awfully sure of himself."

"Yes, awfully."

I hung around till lunch and bought another beer and dug into the meats and bread and cakes and went off and found myself a table—the same one the lawman had been reading his newspaper at—and sat there eating and sipping my beer like I owned the place. I counted out my money. I was down to seventeen dollars and two bits. Add to that the fifty I planned on winning and I'd be aces once again. Figured maybe I'd sell my horse and saddle and buy a train ticket to California and put both my feet in the ocean just to say I did and then look around for some real opportunity. I heard there was a lot of it out there. These old prairies hadn't shown me anything but the ass end of cows and fence lines and a sea of grass. I didn't even want to think of what it was before I took up punching—the faces of the men I'd killed.

The buffalo was all shot out and the farmers were taking over and it was getting so peaceful, most of it, it was goddamn pitiful. Everybody knew if you wanted to make something of yourself you had to either go east or west.

I sat around till the lunch crowd thinned out again then offered to help the one-armed barkeep put away the leftovers. He paid me by giving me a free beer. I thanked him and he poured himself one while four old boys with long beards played dominoes at a table and told each other jokes and laughed and shuffled their ivory.

"So you think you might know somewhere I could land a little work?" I said.

"You like whores?"

"I never held anything against them but me," I said.

"Pink Huston is looking for a bouncer at his cat-house."

"Shit, wasn't exactly what I had in mind as a career move."

"Career move?" He laughed like hell and swiped the beer foam from his moustaches.

"You know what something like that pays, bouncing at his hog farm?"

He shrugged. "You'd have to ask Pink but I imagine, knowing him, he'd want you to take some of your wages out in trade with his gals."

"Where do I find him?"

"You see them railroad tracks just south of here when you rode in?"

"Yeah, I seen them."

"That's where he is. Marshal keeps all the for-sale pussy across those tracks—the dead line, he calls it. Crib whores, Chinese whores, all of 'em. Chalk's got the biggest hog farm within a hundred miles of here. You can't miss it—look for the one with the mansard roof."

I thanked him and went out and mounted my horse and rode down toward the railroad tracks. I could see a line of shacks and one structure with a mansard roof that looked like it belonged north of the tracks, not south. It loomed above the others. The horse was skittish about crossing over the tracks. I patted his neck in a gentle way and said, "Hell, old son, we been south of tracks like these before."

I rode down the one and only street and noticed a lot of the whores had hung out their laundry by draping their underthings and bed-sheets over railings, and some were washing clothes in big galvanized tubs set out front of the cathouses. Several of the ladies were sitting lounging around on porches and balconies— the places that had balconies—in their bloomers, and smoking cigarettes and chatting like school-girls.

Most of them whooped and called out to me when I passed by. I made it a point to pass by slowly.

"Hey cowboy, come on in!"

"Hidey Lonesome."

"I could sure use a good man like you, honey."

"Hey you tall drink of water, come and see Alice!"

Some stuck their rumps out and slapped them just to show me the product. I let it cross my mind briefly that whoremaster might not be a bad profession.

I smiled and touched my hat brim and tried not to think of all that temptation as I rode down to the end place with the mansard roof. There were girls lounging around on the porch there too, four or five of them, and one had a black cat sitting on her lap she was petting. When I dismounted and tied off my horse at the hitch post and stepped up onto the porch she lifted her sloe eyes to me and said, "You like my pussy, honey?" The cat purred contentedly, its eyes closed.

"It's a real fine-looking pussy, ma'am," I said, and the other girls laughed and so did the one holding the cat.

"I'm here to see Pink Huston," I said.

"Pink's inside. But he can't do you half as much good as these girls can."

I leaned over and scratched the cat's head and its ears twitched and I said, "Probably not," and went inside.

It was like something out of the Arabian nights —lots of red damask and heavy wine-colored drapes, settees with carved wood feet, and even a crystal chandelier. A man in spats was sitting at a small burl-wood desk counting money.

34

"You Pink Huston?"

"Who'd be needing to know?" He had an English accent.

"Barkeep over at the Bison Club said you might need a bouncer."

"You any good with your dukes, mate?"

"I'll find out just how good tonight," I said. "I'm going down to Bucky's Corral and sign up to fight Gentleman Harry Ford."

The man stopped counting. "You ever see that bloke fight—Gentleman Harry?"

"No."

"He's a first-class pugilist," he said. "D'ya even know what a pugilist is, lad?"

"I'm from Nebraska, not China," I said.

His laugh sounded like someone strangling a chicken, and he went back to counting.

"What about the job?" I said.

"We'll see how ya do tonight, then I'll decide whether you're the bloke for me."

"Fine," I said. "How much for the one out front with the cat?"

"Lorri? She's not fer sale, laddie. She's me personal snatch."

"We'll talk later then," I said. "After I knock out the Gentleman."

"Yar," he said. "After you coldcock him, eh."

I went out and got on my horse and Lorri stroked her pussy while giving me that look you'd expect a woman with her talents would

35

give and I touched my brim and said, "Destiny is a funny thing, ain't it, ma'am?"

"What do you mean?" she said.

"I think you and I have a date with destiny—that it's something that was bound to happen since before either of us was born."

"Careful, cowboy, Pink is a jealous man, especially when it comes to smooth talkers."

"Yeah, me too," I said, and reined the horse around and headed back across the tracks.

I killed the rest of that afternoon by taking a long soak at a small bathhouse run by a Celestial while waiting to get my clothes cleaned at his laundry in back. Then I got a shave before heading back to the saloon, and nursed a beer or two until the evening hour of seven o'clock, when I walked down to Bucky's Corral. A sizable crowd had gathered.

I stepped up to the corral, which was set up as a boxing ring, and saw the touted Gentleman Harry Ford standing on the other side wearing tight britches with a red sash around his waist. He was bare-chested, no doubt to show off his muscular frame. He had short-cropped black hair and black handlebar moustaches and looked cool as a block of ice as his gaze swept the crowd, no doubt seeing future broken noses, split lips, and busted teeth. A short bald man stood next to him, rubbing Harry's upper arms and shoulders and talking to him, the fighter tilting

36

his head to hear better what the man was telling him, rolling his broad shoulders. Another man stood in the middle of the corral with a megaphone, telling everyone that Gentleman Harry was ready for the first challenger and anyone who had not yet signed up should see him.

"Come on, now, who will be the first to challenge the champeen?" the fellow with the megaphone asked, and a well-built man climbed over the top of the corral and jumped down into the dust and said, "Me."

Somebody standing next to me said the challenger was the town blacksmith—Andy Toe.

"Old Andy will hit him like a mule kicked him," the fellow said. I sure as hell hoped old Andy wouldn't knock the Gentleman out before I got my chance to win the fifty dollars.

"I'll take five on the champeen," I said, and the fellow said, "You're on."

The two fighters were called to the center of the ring while the megaphone fellow gave them instructions about no hitting below the belt, no gouging of eyes or biting off ears. Then he nodded at the bald man who rang a dinner bell, and the blacksmith rushed out to meet the champ and threw a haymaker that the Gentleman ducked easy and as he came up, slammed a right hand to the side of the smith's head that collapsed him like he'd been shot. The megaphone man who had now turned referee counted the smith out, and some other men came and dragged him out of the ring by his arms. I took my five dollars from the kid next to me. He didn't look quite so sure now.

"Who's next?" the referee said.

The kid raised his hand, then got into the corral. He was tall and wiry as a terrier, with little blond hairs on his upper lip.

"Yer mudder know yer fighting?" the referee said jokingly. The boy nodded, and you could see he was nervous the way he shifted his weight from foot to foot like he was dancing on a dime, trying to make it give change.

The man with the dinner bell struck it with a hammer and the boy began to dance around the Gentleman, who more or less stalked the kid, waiting for him to throw a punch. The crowd began to boo the poor exhibition, and the Gentleman stopped and stood there waiting for the kid to do something, to come close enough. Finally the kid got up nerve enough to throw a long looping right hand that hit the Gentleman on the side of his face. They both seemed surprised.

It went like that for a few minutes or so—the kid dancing, throwing slaps against the placid face of the Gentleman, the Gentleman standing there taking it, letting the kid get more and more confidence up until at last he moved in close enough and the Gentleman snapped a straight right hand that landed flush in the center of the kid's puss, snapping his head back like he'd been assassinated. The blow knocked him straight back and dumped him into the trampled dirt and horseshit. The kid sat with his legs splayed out in front of him and spit teeth and waved his feeble hand in resignation. The crowd laughed and booed at the same time.

"Next!" came the call, and a succession of local oafs took their turn with the Gentleman, who knocked each one out, or hit them so hard they quit.

Finally I figured it was as good a time as any and climbed over the top rail and dropped down and paid my money to the referee as he gave me the same instructions about not biting or gouging or hitting in the nutsack. I took off my clean shirt and hung it on the top rail and waited for the dinner bell to ring.

I noticed Pink Huston and Lorri, the cat woman, in the crowd; I wanted to ask if she'd brought her pussy along but this was no time for joking around. I looked down just then and saw some bloody teeth lying in the dirt.

The bell rang and I came in fast and low and popped Gentlemen Harry Ford with a couple of hard left hooks to his short ribs and moved out just as he dropped his own left hand down, grazing my ear and causing it to feel like it had been stung by a wasp.

"Ah, we've got a true lad, now don't we?" he said, grinning so some of his gold teeth showed.

I feinted with a right and threw another hard little hook into his ribs sameplace and saw how that affected him. Some of the smile went off his face. Everybody wants to knock you out in a fistfight, so they try and hit you in the head. But the body is a bigger target and can't move out of the way easy as the head does. A lot like when you have to shoot a man—you aim for the biggest target.

The Gentleman was quick of foot and moved well and came in and hit me with a couple of shocking blows that mostly glanced off my arms, which helped to soften their power, and several off my shoulders as I turned to give more of an angle. I knew I couldn't go long with him; he was a pro and would figure me out, and my teeth would end up with those of the others.

He moved in, his hand already cocked, and I sidestepped just as he threw a fist that whistled past my face. I bent and hooked two more hard lefts into his ribs, same place as before, and I thought I heard something crack. He threw a wild overhand that clipped the back of my head and bounced off my shoulder blade. I staggered like I was hurt and he moved in fast, ready to make the kill, and I brought a right uppercut from down near the border that caught him just under his chin. I put my full weight behind it and it was like hitting rock and I heard him give a hard grunt as his teeth clashed. The blow had caught him completely unawares and stopped him in his tracks, which was all I needed as I smashed a sharp left cross to the bridge of his nose, smashing it like a strawberry hit with a hammer.

He staggered back and I moved in fast, hitting him with as many rights and lefts as I could wing, driving him back and back and back until he was up against the railings and I could feel that handsome face giving way, bones and flesh softening—like hitting a grapefruit—with every blow. Then his eyes rolled up in his head and I stepped back and watched him collapse to his knees before falling facedown in the dirt.

The referee took his time about counting the Gentleman out but the crowd got on him and finally he did and then reached in his pocket and gave me the fifty dollars. I went and put it in my shirt before realizing I had a cut over my left eye that dripped blood, which I temporarily stopped by pressing the heel of my hand to it.

Pink Huston came up then and said, "I lost a hundred dollars on you. Come around later and we'll talk about your job duties."

Lorri slipped me a silk hankie when Pink turned his back to walk away. She gave me a wink. "Mr. Destiny," she said.

City Marshal Chalk Bronson found me as I

41

was holding Lorri's hankie to my face and feeling flush with the new money and the scent of her whorish perfume. Something about a good fight makes a man want to drink and have sex.

"Hell of a fight," he said.

"You lose money on me too?"

"No," he said. "I bet on you."

"Why?"

"I get hunches about people," he said, and then, "Come on, I'll buy you a drink at the Bison. I've got something I want to discuss with you."

CHAPTER THREE

He'd been a worried man looking for an answer he did not think existed. Then he saw the stranger and took note of him and as soon as the stranger started to speak, saying how he was looking for work, and Chalk began to have hope, that this man might be the answer.

So he took careful study of him there in the Bison, saw the way he carried himself, the way he seemed to take note of everything in the place, unafraid to state his case. And the lawman noticed something else too—the bulk that was under the linen duster riding the stranger's right hip.

And when Bill mentioned about the fight, the

stranger didn't hesitate. A man like that, who doesn't hesitate, was just the sort of man Chalk figured he needed. Lately he had felt very alone. Saddled with a problem he couldn't tell anyone about, even his Nora. A secret about a woman you once loved was not something you talked to your wife about. And this particular secret was full of danger for everyone.

So he went on about his business after observing the stranger and suggesting directly that the stranger would be smart to save his money and not put himself in the ring with a professional prizefighter, because more than anything he wanted to see how the stranger would react to such negative comments. It hadn't even fazed him. And so Chalk Bronson thought there was one more test before he made his pitch to the stranger—to watch him actually fight.

That little traveling show had come into town the night before and set up a tent just outside the town's limits, and he had gone out and looked them over. The fighter, himself, this Gentleman Harry Ford, sat eating an apple as calmly as a horse while his manager scurried about directing the local men he'd hired to put up the tent, his face red as the apple his fighter was eating.

Chalk warned them both not to *skin* the locals and that he expected everything to be on the up

43

and up. Sure, sure, the little man said. "My boy's a pro. We don't need to skin nobody."

Chalk told them both he'd be at the fight keeping an eye on things, and the little man did not object, but seemed rather pleased that the local law itself would be in attendance and said, "I don't suppose you'd be putting up the dukes with the Gentleman here?"

"No," said Chalk. "I only fight when it is necessary and not for the sport of it," and went home with his mind still troubled about what had happened earlier in the day when the two punchers had ridden out from Johnny Waco's with the letter of demand that said he had till Friday to make it happen. The letter fully stated what the consequences for him and the town were if he failed to deliver. They were dusty, horse-smelling punchers, the sort he was more used to arresting and throwing in jail for drunk and disorderly than from taking any sort of orders from. But they were fully aware of their own immunity, being the hires of Johnny Waco.

So he went down the night of the fight to watch the stranger, to see if his backbone and fists matched the rest of his confident manner, and placed a ten dollar side bet on him, believing himself a better judge of the human character than most. Then he stood and watched as the Gentleman quickly dispatched his first half-dozen opponents, if they could even be called that, with professional ease and blows that struck the unschooled like hammers.

Then the stranger got into the ring and it was a different story, and Chalk felt vindicated and blessed all at the same time when he saw the stranger was no stranger to using his fists and nerve, and he went home that evening feeling the slightest ray of hope in an otherwise dark world.

Chalk convinced himself that the stranger had arrived when he did for a reason. What else could explain it? Chalk Bronson was not a God-fearing man in the normal sense, but he didn't disbelieve in good fortune either. He believed it was more than just dumb luck that had thus far kept him from getting assassinated in a profession where assassination was not uncommon.

And so he had approached the stranger after the fight and offered to buy him a celebratory drink and then lay out his proposal.

The stranger listened as Chalk told him the deal.

The stranger listened with interest.

"A job's a job," he said to the stranger.

"No it isn't—not always."

"You need money, I'm offering you a good bit of money. More than you can make prizefighting or doing anything else this little burg has to offer."

For Chalk Bronson knew one thing that was common to most men—money, and that everyone had a price. All you had to do was learn what their price was.

The stranger didn't seem to be any different in that way.

CHAPTER FOUR

The barkeep chipped me off a chunk of ice from a block he kept out back to keep his beer barrels cold and put it in a cloth and I held it against my face.

"You knocked that sucker out like you owned him," he said.

"Trick is to keep moving and keep throwing punches," I said. "Some days you get lucky."

Marshal Bronson stood sipping his coffee and listening.

"You said you had something you wanted to discuss with me," I said.

"You found work yet?"

"Yes, I think so. Pink Huston offered me a bouncer job at his hog farm."

"Let's set over there," he said, pointing with his chin to an empty table.

We carried our drinks over and set down and he took off his derby and set it on the empty seat between us and I could see he was losing his hair though still a young man, younger than me, I guessed, by a few years.

"Here's the thing," he said. "I need me a man to do me a special service."

"What sort of service?"

His eyes glanced up toward the bar and then around the room—the place was nearly full that hour, men still talking about the prizefight, working girls, horses, their wives, the weather.

"What I'm going to tell you, you need to keep to yourself. Can I trust you on that regard?"

"Sure," I said.

He reached in his waistcoat pocket, took out a folded piece of paper and unfolded it and said, "You learn to read somewhere along the line, did you?"

It wasn't an insult the way I saw it, just a legitimate question. Lots of fellows dropped out of school before they learned to read, and some never went.

"This arrived yesterday in the noon mail," he said.

I read what was written:

You have one week to return my Antonia or I will come with plenty enough men and burn your town and kill anyone who tries to stop me.
J.W.

"Who is she?" I asked. "Who's he?"

"*He* is Johnny Waco—biggest damn rancher in this part of the state. *She* is his wife and currently an employee of Pink Huston—your future employer."

"Why doesn't he just come and get her, he wants her back?"

"Long story," he said. "Just that it is my town and I'm responsible for seeing it doesn't get burned down. It's what I get paid to do."

"Where do I fit into all this?"

"I want to hire you to help me deliver her to him."

"Me? Shit, what'd I do to piss you off?"

"That your idea of humor?"

"No, seriously, why me?"

"Like I told you, I get hunches about people. My hunch is you'd be a good man to have on my side."

"Good and dead, I reckon, if the threat in that letter holds any water and you can't get Waco's wife back to him."

"How's five hundred dollars sound?"

"I miss something about this place?" I said. "I never met a lawman yet who made over thirty a month."

"Special case," he said. "I can get the money."

"What makes you think I'm any sort of man for this?"

He looked at the butt of the Merwin Hulbert riding my hip.

"The way you wear that hogleg," he said. "Like a man that can use it."

"Could be I just want folks to think that."

"Well, do you know how to use it?"

"Yeah," I said. "I do. Don't mean I will, though."

He eased back in his chair.

"You're half as good with a gun as you are your fists then you're worth the money."

I weighed my options. I could turn him down and go bounce drunks and peckerwoods at the hog farm and probably get plenty of free quim for my troubles as well as a steady paycheck, or I could make a lot of money fast and probably get killed before I could spend it. Or I could get on my horse and ride the hell out of there and forget I ever heard of Coffin Flats. Thing with the bouncer job was, if this Waco *did* come riding in with a bunch of men and burned the town to the ground, my bouncer job would get burned with it, especially if Waco's wife was working for Pink. So that was no good. Leaving was probably the smartest thing to do—after all, I had over sixty dollars in my pocket. But five hundred sounded like a lot more than sixty if I remembered the mathematics right I'd learned in a West Texas schoolhouse when I wasn't daydreaming about girls, horses, and fighting Indians.

"Who else you got to help you on this?" I said. "I mean if things don't work out getting Waco's wife back to him?"

"Got two deputies I don't know if I can count on."

"Maybe you should fire them then and get you someone you can count on."

"I don't want to sit around here bullshittng, Mr. Glass. You're either in or out. We can't pull this off, this whole town is going to burn and maybe a few good folks will die."

"Including you."

"I'm not afraid to die," he said. "I've been close to it a dozen times already. But I got this sick wife . . ."

"I get the five hundred either way it turns out —long as I'm around to collect it?"

"Either way long as you don't cut and run."

"So if we can get the woman and deliver her to Waco, we're aces."

"That's the size of it."

"Where's this old boy's place?"

"A full day's ride from here."

"Why the hell doesn't he just come and get her is the question bothering me. The one you says got a long story behind it. I don't mind putting my neck on the line long as I know what I'm putting it there for."

Chalk sipped his coffee and stared into the cup.

"Because he wants *me* to do it."

"You want to level with me or just sit here pulling my dally rope?"

"It's complicated," he said.

"I already figured as much. How *is* it complicated?"

"Antonia and I were engaged to be married once—a long time ago, before she met Waco. But I went off to fight in that goddamn war because I thought it was my duty and I got hurt and lost in my head and didn't come back when I could have. I was gone two years longer than the war lasted. And when I *did* come back, she was with Waco. She thought I was killed—lots of men were and their families never knew it. Waco had money and could provide her a life I couldn't even think about even if I had come back—"

Somebody shouted from across the room and Chalk looked up suddenly, saw it wasn't anything but some drunk being a drunk.

"Sounds like maybe you didn't lose all that much in losing her."

He looked at me hard then.

"You don't know anything about her," he said.

"You're right, I don't. So Waco took up with her, but how the hell did it go from that to where she's at now—moonlighting at Pink Huston's hog farm?"

"Time I come back here, I was a drunk myself,

51

rundown and wasted. She was married to Waco. I met Nora and she pulled me out of the bottle and I hired on as a deputy, stayed sober, and when the marshal quit, I was offered the job. Thing is, I'd run into Antonia now and then when she'd come to town. We'd talk—privately. She wanted me back. I told her I couldn't, even though I was still weak when it came to her. I messed up this once with her and later she told me she was pregnant with my child. I said I was sorry, I'd do what I could but I wasn't leaving Nora. She tried to kill herself but all she managed to do was kill the child with the poison she drank. Afterward she got hooked on the laudanum Doc gave her to keep her sedated—found out she liked the world better when she wasn't sober. When she couldn't get laudanum, she got into opium and booze. Christ! I have to explain all this to you?"

"I can pretty much guess the rest. Pink kept her in dope in exchange for her working for him."

"Yeah, that's pretty much it."

"I still don't get why Waco just doesn't come and shoot Pink and take her back."

"He blames me, thinks I run a game on her to get her to leave him. She must have told him about the child. Believes if I hadn't come back, none of this would have happened. He's probably right, none of it would have happened. He wants to embarrass me, make me pay for my sins—show her what sort of no account I am."

"Why not just tell him to go to hell?"

" 'Cause I never mentioned any of this to Nora, for one thing. Now she's sick, and if I lose her, I've got nothing to live for. And for another, I've swore to protect these folks and this town. I guess as much as I messed up, I owe somebody something."

I studied on it and what I saw was a worried man—but worried more about others than himself—and I knew all about that, having been down that road myself a time or three.

"It sounds like a lot more than wanting to embarrass you," I said. "It sounds like pure revenge."

"Yeah," he said. "It does, but so what?"

"No matter what, you lose."

"Probably so."

"You could always take your wife and just ride away and not look back."

"That wouldn't end nothing. He'd come and burn this town and then he'd come after me. He just wants me to grovel awhile before he puts his boot on the back of my neck. Maybe I give him back what he wants he'll let things go. Then Nora and I can leave and find someplace to ourselves."

"Tell you what," I said. "I'm supposed to go see Pink about that job. Let me go see what I can find out with regards to Antonia. Then I'll find you and see we can't work something out."

"You want the job or no?"

"Yeah. Maybe."

"I should go over there with you."

"And do what?"

His gaze dropped to his coffee cup; a small black mirror that reflected a troubled face.

"Where can I find you when I come back?"

"I'll be right here."

I stood and went out into the cool night. You could feel the seasonal change, and the sky looked like it had holes poked in it with silver pins. I rode down to the railroad tracks—the dead line—and could see the lights on in some of the bagnios and crib joints. Behind those doors and walls and windows, there was some serious action going on and everybody was playing the hand they'd been dealt.

I tied off in front to Pink's place and knocked on the door and it was answered by the woman, Lorri. She was wearing a green silk dress and holding that same cat.

"You come back to play with my pussy?" she said, smiling, stroking the fur between the cat's ears. The way she said it made me want to.

"I've always been a cat lover," I said.

She smiled and held the door wide for me to come in, and there were several women of various ages and sizes lounging on the furniture. Pink was there at his little desk, dressed in a silk smoking jacket and smoking a cheroot like some Arab sheik watching over his harem.

"Ah, the pugilist," he said. "Y've come for the job then, laddie?"

"Tonight," I said, "I've come simply for the pleasure."

"Certainly, take yer pick—anyone but me and Lorri, that is." The two of them exchanged looks.

"Somebody told me that a gal named Antonia was a good choice," I said.

"Ah, right you are. Step forward, my angel, the man has requested your services."

A thin strawberry blonde lifted herself unsteadily from one of the horsehair divans and wobbled forward. She was pretty, with a thin emaciated face and dark shadows under both eyes and hollow cheeks, and I'd bet a dollar she used to be a lot more attractive.

"Tell you what," Pink said. "It's on the house tonight, in spite of what you cost me already. Just to show you I'm a generous bloke."

She took me by the hand and we went up a carpeted stair to a room that was narrow with striped wallpaper. The flame from a small lamp by the bedside danced inside the glass chimney.

"What's your pleasure, cowboy?" she said without the least bit of enthusiasm, and began to undress from the robe she was wearing. The robe fell away and what was left was a too thin woman with sallow flesh covering her ribs and bony hips. I picked up the robe and wrapped her in it.

"Hey . . ."

"I just want to talk to you," I said.

She sat wearily on the side of the bed. "You got anything to drink?"

"No."

"I could use a cigarette."

"I don't smoke," I said.

"Jesus, what are you, a damn priest?"

She rested her face in her palms.

"I came to see you on behalf of Chalk Bronson," I said.

She looked up, her eyes red, tired, half closed. "What's *he* want?"

"He needs to take you back to Johnny Waco."

"Yeah, like hell."

"Look, you've got the man between a rock and a hard place, miss."

Her mouth twisted with displeasure.

"Cowboy, what I do is fuck, I don't talk, and I don't care if he's between a rock and a mountain." She started to rise but I put a hand on her shoulder and pushed her back down again.

"Waco is going to burn the town down if the marshal doesn't bring you to him," I said.

She looked at me like I wasn't there.

"Well, it's going to be a tough place to make a living then," she said. "Because no way in hell am I going back to Johnny Waco."

"Can I ask you something?"

She shrugged. "Why not."

"You happy with this situation?"

She looked at the flame dancing in the glass chimney of the lamp, the light catching in her eyes.

"It beats living with Johnny Waco."

"I can make it better."

"How?"

So I told her the plan—the one I'd just made up there on the spot. The one that was mostly desperate and probably would get me killed and maybe her too. But what the hell were the choices? Okay, so I knew I could still ride away and not look back. But it isn't always that simple. Maybe if I'd never known what would happen, it could have been easier, but now I knew and I'd have to live with it—whatever I did or didn't do for a very long time. And if I could pull something off that maybe saved some lives, maybe a lot of lives, then maybe it was worth a try.

When I finished telling her, she said, "You call that a plan?"

CHAPTER FIVE

She had been waiting forever it seemed.

First there was the wait for him to come home again from the war. And when he didn't, there was the wait of mourning. The wait of mourning was followed by wait for light to come into her life again after all the long lonely dark nights.

Then came the wait for new love, if there was such a thing.

It had not come exactly as she had hoped. But then what great love could repeat itself?

Johnny Waco wooed her. He was wealthy and in some ways larger than life. But he was a great mystery to her as well. He had a reputation as a hard man without forgiveness toward his enemies, and later he would prove to be a man who kept his secrets secret, a man of interminable silence. But in the beginning of his courtship, he showed her none of that. He arrived in carriages pulled by pretty horses and took her for long rides and showed her the width and breadth of his holdings.

He arranged picnics beneath large cottonwoods that guarded clear running creeks and rivers. He could be wildly generous and often was. He once bought her a hat on a whim—a hat she knew she'd never wear—that he'd ordered from a catalogue simply because he thought she would like it. It had ostrich feathers.

He let her know from the outset his intentions to marry her. He professed his love and his desire for her. Even if he wasn't Chalk Bronson, it was still flattering in a way.

There was no one else that came even close to being marriageable. Just old men, punchers, gamblers, the occasional drummer selling tinware or elixirs from the back of a medicine show wagon.

She'd told him no at first, said she wasn't ready for marriage. Her heart still longed for the man who'd gone away and never came home again. Dead, lost, disfigured, out of his mind? She couldn't be sure. No word had come. He had been simply swallowed by a distant war she only read about in the newspaper. Time left her without answers.

Johnny Waco was a force in his own right. Tall and good-looking with smoke-dark eyes, a man who did not hesitate to brag that he always got what he was after.

He seemed just decent enough, and after a time her resistance broke down; it was easier to marry him then to keep finding reasons not to. They were wed in the church by the priest even though Johnny made no claim to any particular religious belief. He would do what was right by her. And afterward there was a huge wedding feast prepared by his hired help, Maria Montero, his housekeeper, and her husband, Pedro, along with some of the hired hands who carried out long tables into the yard for guests to sit at, decorated with white crepe.

They took the train to San Francisco for a honeymoon.

The ocean startled her. The ships in the harbor seemed to be waiting to take her to exotic places. Weeks after their return to the desert she could still hear the creak of ropes, see the lighthouse light floating on the black water at night. The hotels in San Francisco had electric lights.

Their lovemaking was for her the hardest part. She still remembered the hands of Chalk Bronson, the scent of his skin, the landscape of his body. Everything with Johnny Waco was different, hurried, and in the end unpleasant. She told herself she would give it time, that she could not expect him to be her late lover. Men are as different as horses are different, as the days are different, the seasons.

But time did not ease her unease around him. And by the time of their return home again, she felt as if he found pleasure in her for only one reason.

His personal bar is where she developed her taste for liquor—a glass in the early afternoon relaxed her. Another at supper made the long hours leading to bedtime seem less dull. Later she would learn to calm her mind after he had fallen asleep by going to the cabinet and pouring herself a glass of brandy. It made her feel less stained.

After two years of this new but unhappy life she heard news that nearly stopped her heart: Chalk Bronson had suddenly appeared in town. It was exactly as though a dead man had risen from the grave—the shock of it.

She fought the urge to go and seek him out. Her husband warned her against such indiscretions.

"If he thinks he's come back for you," he said, "he's badly mistaken."

She vowed that she no longer could love a man who would abandon her for so long. How could she? Posing such a question to Johnny Waco seemed to calm him.

But then she went. And she found him staggering drunk down the street. She hardly recognized him. His face was haggard, his cheeks hollow and grizzled with graying beard. He'd lost a great deal of weight. He wore moustaches long and unkempt.

He seemed just as surprised to see her.

They were formal at first, like strangers being introduced. Her heart ached to touch him and make him new again. He ended up weeping into his rough beard.

"I'm sorry," he said over and over.

Whatever they had once had was broken and they both knew it.

She rushed home and locked herself in her room and wept. She'd never felt such anguish. And that afternoon she got fully and maddeningly drunk for the first time, and her husband found her huddled in the corner of the room raving in her anguish.

"You saw him, didn't you? Against my wishes, you saw him!"

She didn't bother to try and explain.

He warned her again to stay away.

"Will you beat me if I do not?" she said.

"No, but I will beat him in ways you will not like."

The next time she went to town she planned carefully, waiting until he had gone away on a cattle buying trip.

She learned where Chalk Bronson was staying, which room at the hotel, and went up the back stairs and knocked on his door, and he opened it, standing there wearing just his trousers, his hair tousled, his eyes red and anguished.

He let her in and they talked.

Their talking eased them beyond many of the old barriers that had been built up in his absence. He confessed he still loved her. She asked him why he hadn't come home after the war.

"I can't explain it," he said. "It changed me. I felt like I'd lost myself. I needed to find who I had once been and went in search of it. I couldn't bring myself home to you the way I was. You wouldn't have cared for what I'd become."

His truth became her own. She ordered the copper tub brought up the room and filled with hot water and soap and towels.

"I want to wash you," she said to the man who should have been her husband. She did not know if he legally still was, but in her heart he still was.

He stripped, and she could see how pale his skin was, how thin he'd become, the ridge of bone in the center of his back as he bent to get into the tub. She took the bar of the soap into her hands and delicately began to wash him, his back and shoulders and neck. He closed his eyes. She washed his hair and rinsed it and he sat there with his eyes closed. For her it was like washing away their sins, past and present.

"I heard you married Johnny Waco," he said, his eyes still closed.

She told him why she had. He asked if she was happy.

"Do you think I would be here if I was?"

He reached up across his chest and laid his hand on her damp wrist and held it there on his shoulder.

"There is someone I've met," he said.

"I don't want to know who it is."

He told her the woman's name was Nora Hancock. She worked in the dry goods store. "She's a widow," he said.

She knew who the woman was, had seen her often when she'd shopped at the mercantile. A rather plain woman of quiet disposition. She tried not to compare herself with this Nora, this widow.

"It doesn't matter," she said.

"It does."

Then for the first time in three years they kissed, and it was like the very first time they kissed, as though nothing had been forgotten or left out. Certain things do not change.

Later they lay on the bed together. The room quiet except for a man coughing next door.

She knew then she'd been changed, that he had put new life into her. She did not say this; it was a secret she would keep for a little while longer until she was sure. She kissed his rough hands.

"Are you sorry?" she asked.

"I think I've dishonored us both."

"No, you haven't. I came because I wanted to see you. I wanted to erase the past, to start again. I hated you after I saw you the other day. I've hated you for three years. I told myself I could never not hate you. But it isn't true, Chalk. No matter what you might do to me, I can't hate you."

He didn't know how to tell her he'd changed, that his love for her had changed.

"I'm not the same man," is what he said, hoping she'd read into it the truth of who he was now.

Someone knocked on the door. They lay together silently. The knock came again, followed by a woman's voice asking if he was in there. He looked at her but did not answer. Then they heard footsteps fading.

"That was her," he said. "That was Nora."

"You could have answered it," she said.

"No, I couldn't have."

"You're ashamed of me?"

"No. I just wouldn't want to shame her."

She wasn't sure of where she stood with him now. It would take time, she told herself, to make things back to where they once were. She would ask for a divorce. She knew what she wanted. But something warned her not to he too hasty. Something in his voice, his not answering the knock at the door, warned her against rushing to a decision.

And then weeks later when she broke the news she was pregnant and saw the look in his eyes, the near sadness, she understood that he would not marry her.

It was like someone slamming shut a door suddenly in the middle of the night, a sound that both startles and has finality.

"You have to understand," he said. "I've given

my love to Nora. She has been good and kind to me, she has saved me from maybe killing myself. I couldn't let her down by leaving her . . ."

"Yes," she said magnanimously, even though her chest felt crushed. "Of course you couldn't."

"I'll do what's necessary, of course," he said. "As far as the baby is concerned."

"No. There is no need to trouble yourself with it," she said, and left and went back to the ranch of her husband and found his liquor and drank it until she couldn't stand.

Every day after was like that, and Johnny Waco would find her in bed late in the afternoons. He thought she had a sickness until he discovered the hidden empty bottles. He assigned Maria to watch after her, to keep her away from the liquor. But by then she'd become quite clever in getting it and hiding it.

A fall caused her to begin bleeding.

Dr. Flax declared she had a miscarriage.

"Your husband should be here with you," he said.

"No, he doesn't know," she said. "And I'd ask that you not tell him."

"Of course, of course."

She went and packed a few things and left the following day. If she was to be what she thought herself as, a whorish person, there was only one man in town who could make her such. Pink Huston.

They worked out an agreement over a pipe of opium. He called it "chasing the dragon."

He said, "You have lovely breasts, Antonia."

She closed her eyes as his hands sought her out.

"This is the first test," she remembered him saying.

After that it no longer mattered.

CHAPTER SIX

I told her to think about it, that I planned on taking a room at the hotel and if she was agreeable to come see me in the morning. She looked at me like I was asking for a line of credit.

"Just think about it before you say no," I said.

"What about the other thing?"

"You mean what I paid for? I didn't pay for it, you were a gift."

I saw the look in her eyes, that of being used to the lowest level, and knew I'd driven in a wedge to pry her loose from this place, the pimp out in the other room.

"Come see me in the morning, unless you like being treated like this."

As I walked out and past the parlor, Pink Huston called, "Well, laddie, how was it?"

"Worth every penny," I said. He laughed at the joke.

"What about that job offer?"

"I'll let you know tomorrow." Lorri was there with him, draped over him like a wounded angel. She and Pink both had dreamy looks. I'd seen that look in other eyes. There was an opium pipe there on the stand next to them and the room smelled sweet. I went out and rode back over the tracks under a night pinpricked with stars.

I found Chalk still there at the Bison.

"Well?" he said.

"I might have a plan."

"You want to let me in on it?"

"I won't know for sure until tomorrow morning if it's actually a plan that might work."

He ran his fingers through the threads of his hair.

"And if your plan doesn't work out?"

"I've got a backup plan."

"I'd never have taken you for a planner."

"Looks can be deceiving."

"That's not what I meant."

"How sure are you about raising that five hundred?" I said.

"Then you're accepting my offer?"

"Maybe."

"I can probably have it tomorrow. I need to talk to the city council."

"Then I'll see you tomorrow."

"Where?"

"I'll find you."

He stood and put on his derby and patted the crown, then strode out, leaving the doors swinging behind him. Nobody seemed to notice his departure. In fact everyone seemed to be enjoying themselves. It seemed like just any other night in a bar with men drinking in it and I thought about the way people are before a bad storm they don't know is coming, the kind of storm that brings a cyclone down on them and tears the shit out of everything in its path, killing people and animals, the guilty and innocent alike. They are always oblivious until it's too late. I understood and respected Chalk Bronson for not panicking the townsfolk with his lament.

I went and found a hotel room at a place with the word Hotel painted on its face. Simple, the way I prefer it. Not the Coffin Flats Hotel, or anything pretentious, just *Hotel.*

An old man under an eyeshade sitting behind the desk reading a book peered over his spectacles when I came in.

"Need a room," I said.

"Front or back?"

"Back," I said.

"Got none in the back. Give you one in the front."

"Okay, front then."

He pushed the register at me. "Sign your name, please."

"What are you reading?" I said, curious.

"*Don Quixote*," he said.

I'd heard of it.

"Crazy old bastard puts a piss pot on his head and thinks he's a knight," he cackled. "Damnedest story I ever read."

"Sounds interesting. How much for the room?"

"How long you staying?"

"I'm not sure."

"Two dollars a day or ten for a full week. Cheaper by the week, you break it down."

"Let's just do a day at a time."

"Let me know by noon if you're staying another day or if you're not."

I put the money on the counter and he handed me a skeleton key.

"You got a boy who can take my horse over to the livery and get him fed and watered down?"

"He'll be along soon. He's over cross the tracks getting his wick wet. Boy's plum pussy crazy. Ever time he gets a dollar he spends it on one of those crib whores. I tried to warn him he's going to get the pox and go blind someday. You think a randy boy will listen to an old man like me?"

I put another dollar on the desk.

"Tell him to tell the liveryman I'll settle up with him when I come to pick up my horse."

He looked at the name I'd written on the register.

"Mr. Glass." He looked at me. Grinned till his mouth looked like a row of shoe peg corn. "Shit, I know who you are," he said.

"I don't see how, I've never been here before."

"I seen you once in a gunfight in El Paso," he said.

"It's news to me. I never been in El Paso either."

"Yessir, Mr. Hardin," he said. "Far as I'm concerned, you're just Mr. Jim Glass, like it says here."

"Hardin?"

"No sir, I didn't mean nothing by it. Last thing I'd want to do is get on your bad side," the clerk said.

The only Hardin I knew was one called John Wesley—real bad son of a bitch if even half of what I heard about him was true.

"That who you think I am, John Wesley Hardin?"

He raised his hands in supplication.

"No sir, you are whoever you say you are." His raised hands trembled like a pair of leaves in a stiff wind.

"Well, you just keep to your business and we'll get along just fine," I said.

"Yessir."

"Where's my room?"

"Up them stairs, turn left, second door on your left."

When I got up there I set there on the bed and pulled off my boots and then my pants and shirt after setting my Henry rifle in the corner and hanging my gun rig on the bedpost above my pillow, then stretched out and it felt damn good.

John Wesley Hardin. Hmmm. I wondered if the mistake would be any advantage to me or if it would simply inspire somebody to come up and stick a gun in my ear and pull the trigger.

I thought about my plan. I never stole a woman before. Never even tried. Closed my eyes and went to sleep. The one thing I got from reading the Bible, which I did a time or two when I was younger and scared and feeling especially sinful, was that worrying didn't change a hair on your head. I sleep like a dead man.

Knocking at the door awakened me. Morning light fell into the room through a dirty window. I pulled on my pants and opened it. It was the woman, Antonia.

"Come in," I said.

She was dressed in trousers and a coat and had her hair twisted into a braid. She looked wasted, like a puncher home from a three day drunk, but you could still see her former beauty lurking somewhere behind the weary eyes, the hollow cheeks, the grim mouth.

"How do I know I can trust you?" she said after I closed the door. "How do I know you won't just hand me over to him and leave?"

"You ran away once, you can do it again if that's the case."

"Like I said, that's your plan?"

"No, I told you what my plan was."

"He'll kill me," she said.

"If that's his intent, he'll do it anyway if he comes for you. I think all he wants to do is rub Bronson's face in it and drag his name through the mud, show him who's the boss dog."

"He wants to humiliate me just as much."

"You want to do this or not?"

"I could use a drink."

"No, that's the last thing you need."

She looked at me. "The hell you know what I need?"

"You're right, I don't."

"The way I see this is I'm the sacrificial lamb to save this town of do-gooders. Let me tell you something, mister. They're not all good. Half the big shots here have paid me and the other whores Saturday night visits while their wives wait for them at home and then go stand in church Sunday morning like saints. They're no better than those dirty punchers. Why should I care if they get burned out?"

"Maybe not them, but their wives and kids," I said.

I could see how that affected her—the mention of kids.

"Chalk tell you about me and him?"

73

"He did."

"About our child?"

"Yeah, that too."

For the first time I saw a moment of softness in her eyes.

"You know, there's another way out of this," she said.

"If it's a better plan than mine, I'm all ears."

"I could just kill myself."

"Shit, I never thought of that."

"Don't be a wise ass."

"I'm not. But I figure if you did that, it would just piss this Waco off and he'd probably blame it on Chalk like he has everything else, maybe more, and what do you think he'd do then?"

"I guess it wouldn't matter—at least to me it wouldn't if I was dead."

"Give my way a shot and if that don't work I'll loan you my gun."

"You're a hard son of a bitch," she said.

"Yeah, so I've been told."

"We'll see how hard when it comes to Johnny Waco."

"Wait here, I've got to go see Chalk about the money."

"Two hundred and fifty, isn't that what you said?"

"Half of five, yes."

"Not a hell of a lot for a fresh start some-where."

"What were you thinking?"

"Maybe you could get him to squeeze these paper collar saints for more—a thousand or two."

"That's an idea."

Something akin to a smile played at the corner of her mouth.

"We're no different, you and me," she said.

"How so?"

"We're both whores—that's our nature."

"Because we do things for money?"

"Isn't that what being a whore is—selling yourself for money?"

"I guess I never thought of it that way or I'd have charged more along the way."

"Yeah, like anyone would have paid."

"Now who's being a wise ass?"

"Go on before I change my mind."

"See you in a while."

"Yeah," she said, and sat on the bed looking glum.

As I was going past the desk I saw a young fellow with carrot red hair sitting in a chair with his eyes half closed.

"Hey," I said. His eyes went up like sprung window shades.

"Are you the one who took care of my horse last night?"

"Yessir, if you're him."

"Who?"

"Mr. Hardin . . . er, I mean Mr. Glass."

"I am. I just wanted to make sure you took care of my animal."

He nodded, looked scared.

"Don't wet yourself, son."

"You got anything else you want me to do for you, sir?"

"Yeah," I said, and put two dollars on the desk. "Go and get a breakfast and take it to the woman up in my room."

He had front teeth like a rabbit when he grinned.

"She's one of those high-priced ones, ain't she?" he said. "I seen her once or twice coming out of Pink Huston's hog farm."

"She's a guest of mine," I said, "treat her with respect."

"Yes sir."

I walked over to the jail and saw Chalk through the window sitting there at his desk with a cup of coffee looking like he hadn't slept. I opened the door and went in.

"I'll need a thousand instead of five hundred to make your troubles go away," I said.

"Yeah, and I need to be twenty-one again and have all my hair back but that's not going to happen either."

"How do you know—about the thousand, not the hair, I mean—unless you ask?"

"I know these old boys are businessmen, not fools," he said.

76

"Exactly."

"Why the extra?"

"Need half for her."

"Antonia?"

"Yeah."

"I don't get it."

So I told him the plan.

"You call that a plan?" he said.

"Funny, but that's the same thing she said."

"Take her back and then steal her?"

"Yeah, simple, but sometimes simple is better."

"It's a fucking joke."

"Maybe. But what's he want? He wants you to bring her to him so he can make you look bad, like he owns you. But what do you care if you can save this town yourself? You have to ask yourself is it worth it—to look bad in front of her and to drag your reputation through the mud. He's checking your pride, Marshal. Figures once he's ruined your reputation you'll quit and leave. Pride's killed as many men as guns."

I could see the lines deepen in his face.

"Then I what, quit, after he's made me look like a fool?"

"Better quit and looking for another job than the alternative."

"I'm not so sure."

"Nothing else, you've got a wife you say you love, just like these councilmen have got wives they say they love. You lay it out for them—how

77

Waco will come and burn their town down and scatter them like sheep and a thousand will look cheap."

He stood and put on his derby.

"What the hell," he said. "I guess it don't cost nothing to ask," and went out.

I waited till he came back pretty sure none of this was going to come out right. He was right about me, I never was much of a planner. I just did whatever needed doing at the time it needed it. I remember something my old man told me a long time ago: "Don't ever do something just for the money."

Less than an hour and Chalk Bronson was back in the office. He took an envelope from his inside pocket and tossed it on the desk. It looked fat—like a thousand dollars fat.

"Your move," he said.

"I'll go get your ex."

"Leave off with that shit, okay?"

"Okay."

I picked up the envelope and went back up to the hotel. She was sitting there on the bed the same as she had been when I left—the plate of food untouched.

"You should have eaten something," I said.

"What are you, my father?"

"No, but if I was, I'd make you eat something."

I threw the envelope on the bed.

"Count out half and put on your coat."

She looked at it listlessly.

"I need a drink or something." Her hands were trembling as she counted out half the money, folded it and put it in her coat pocket then put the coat on.

"I'll stop at the Bison and pick you up a bottle."

"Thank you," she said, and I felt she really meant it.

"This will work out," I said.

"I don't even care anymore," she said.

I felt like I was leading a lamb to slaughter, looking at her, the sad way she seemed. She reminded me of everything wrong there was about life and little there was right about it.

Don't ever do anything just for the money, Jim.

CHAPTER SEVEN

We walked over to the jail and went in and Chalk was there standing at the window and he looked at her with eyes that were full of some deep sorrow only the two of them knew about.

"Antonia," he said.

She started to speak then didn't.

He looked at me.

"I want to know something," he said.

"Go ahead, we're all friends here, right?"

"I got word you might be John Wesley Hardin."

I had to force myself not to smile. "The kid at the hotel, right? Or the old man."

"Raford," he said. "The old man."

"What if I was, how would that make any difference about what we're doing here?"

He chewed his lower lip. I could see he was armed with a bulldog revolver in a short holster.

"The council knew I just handed over a thousand dollars of their money to John Wesley Hardin, I'd be fired."

"Might be a stroke of good luck for you then, considering."

"I'm not fucking around here, are you or aren't you?"

"No," I said. "Jim Glass, like I told you."

"Shit," he said, and put on his hat and coat. "I rented a buggy, Antonia. I got it pulled around back."

"I thought I'd tag along," I said.

"Suit yourself," he said.

I fell in behind them on the westbound road. Wind blew in our faces, sharp and cold. You could tell it was going to be an unpleasant day, and I had to tug my hat down tight to keep it from blowing off my head and turned up my coat collar. I figured the two of them had some things in private they would probably want to talk over—or maybe not, so I maintained a good distance behind them. At one point, about two hours into the ride, he stopped the buggy and I heard the two of them arguing and saw the bottle I'd bought her go flying. I spurred ahead and said, "There a problem?"

"The fuck you buy her whiskey for?"

"Because she asked for it and looked like she could use it."

She looked at me with half-lidded eyes.

"What the hell do you know about anything?" he said.

"She's entitled," I said, "considering she's putting herself on the line for you, wouldn't you say?"

He lowered his gaze then dismounted the wagon and walked out on the prairie until he found the bottle. He wiped the dead dry grass from it and walked back carrying it in one hand and held it out to her, and she took it and cradled it against her as he climbed back up into the wagon and snapped the reins. We rode on the rest of the day like that and I felt like I was part of something that was not only unkind but downright cruel, and I had to keep thinking about sacrifice. Only it wasn't my sacrifice but hers, and it was easy for you to think about it if it wasn't you doing the sacrificing but someone else. And it didn't make me feel any better by a long shot.

We stopped before the darkness behind us caught us and swallowed us whole.

I said, "I thought it was just a day's ride?"

Chalk said, "It is if you're riding a good horse and not a buggy and hauling a sick woman."

There was a stream that ran crooked as a dog's hind leg through the dying grass, and I gathered pieces of kindling and started a fire while he set up a small pup tent he'd taken from the back of the buggy along with a sack of foodstuff and a coffeepot. She sat there on the ground sipping from the bottle, staring off into the long nothingness and empty places.

Time everything was ready, he scraped her some beans and salted pork onto a plate and held it out to her. She refused it.

"Eat something, please," he said.

"You eat it," she said. "I don't want it."

I got myself a plate and sat back against my saddle and the night folded over us till there was just our shadows playing in and out of the firelight, the flames licking at the night.

"I don't feel good about this," he said to her, the fire between them. "Just so you know."

"Why should you care, Chalk? Why should you care?"

He looked beat in every way a man can look beat.

I ate fast then set the plate aside and laid back and pulled my blanket up around me with my head propped on my saddle and pulled my hat down over my eyes like I was sleeping. I didn't want to be part of their intimacy even if it was conflicted.

"You think we could just not argue?" he said. "Just this once?"

"Yes, Chalk. Our arguing days will be forever over come tomorrow when you hand me over to Johnny."

I thought of all the ways a woman can hurt a man and the ways a man can hurt a woman, and it wasn't like they were trying to hurt each other, they just didn't know how not to anymore.

I waited until everything fell silent for a time before I let myself go to sleep to a low wind moaning over the grass like sorrow itself.

We rose with the daylight and took turns going off into the bushes and had some fresh-made coffee and some bacon and cold biscuit sandwiches—at least he and I did; she still refused to eat anything, and I saw the bottle was empty on the ground next to her blanket. A soft rain began to fall by the time we broke camp and I thought it was just an unpleasant morning. My half of the money wasn't much comfort.

We rode till about mid-morning and then turned off the main road up a wagon trace and followed it for maybe half an hour more till we topped a rise and there in the distance was a windmill turning in the wind and beyond it some buildings.

"That's his place?" I said.

"We've been on his place since last evening," Chalk said. I could see shorthorn cattle scattered all over the grasslands and riders working in among them cutting some out for branding, which was being done down closer to the buildings. Work sort of stopped as we approached; the hired help stood watching us ride up to the main house.

I could see Chalk's features were set hard as stone as we neared, and the woman next to him with her eyes downcast. Three men stood on the porch of the long house.

"Which one's him?" I said.

"The middle one," Chalk said, and my eyes shifted to him.

He was tall and wore his pants stuffed down inside mule ear boots and wore a short coat and a pancake hat. He had a long red scarf tied around his neck and looked like something out of a dime novel. The other two flanking him were heeled with revolvers riding high on their hips and one had a quirt in his left hand and they both stood slouched slightly in that loose way men with bad attitudes will stand.

Chalk halted the buggy a few feet from the porch and nobody said anything, but Johnny Waco was looking at me, trying to assess my reason for being among them, and I didn't flinch because you just didn't do that with the sort of man who knew how powerful he was. The other two took notice of me as well. I had made it a point to unbutton my coat before we got there so they could see I was heeled too and had slid the Henry from its scabbard and rested it across the pommel of my saddle. Best way to keep trouble from happening is to be prepared for it. Let a man know what stuff you're made of so there's no guesswork to it. If it comes anyway, there was no stopping it but with a bullet.

Johnny's eyes finally shifted to the woman.

"Get down from there," he said, "and come here to me."

She started to get down but Chalk laid a hand on her forearm and stopped her.

"I want assurances this is the end of it," he said to Johnny.

Waco cocked his head like a dog that had just heard something it didn't know what it was.

"You get down too, Chalk."

They both got down. I kept an eye on the two who were heeled. Any trouble breaking out would come from them first. Waco didn't look like he was armed, but then you didn't know what he might be wearing under his coat.

"Come up here on the porch," Waco said to the woman. She looked at Chalk then went and climbed up onto the porch and stood there while Waco looked her over like a horse he was considering.

"Go inside," he said. I thought maybe she'd look back at Chalk one more time, but she didn't, just went inside like a beat dog.

"Then it's over," Chalk said.

"No, not quite," Waco said.

"What else?"

Waco's gaze again shifted to me.

"You don't want none of this action, mister."

I noticed some more men had gathered 'round, all of them armed.

"You don't interfere here, or you'll not even have a chance to regret it," he said.

Chalk looked back at me.

"Stay out of this, Glass, no matter what happens."

"You sure?"

"I am."

I slid the Henry back into its scabbard.

Waco nodded his head and three men stepped forward and two of them took Chalk by the arms and the third man took the lawman's bulldog revolver and tossed it in the dirt. I felt something go tight in my guts.

"You know I can't just send you back without folks knowing there is a price to pay for everything when it comes to dealing with me," Waco said. Then he looked at me again and said, "You pay attention here, in case you ever get it in your mind to cross me, mister." I didn't have to look 'round me, behind me, to know that several of the others had drawn their guns and had them aimed at me.

He nodded again and the man who'd taken Chalk's pistol from him slammed a fist into Chalk's ribs, doubling him over, then crashed another blow to his chin, knocking him to his knees even as he was being held up by the two men holding him by the arms.

It was a hard thing to watch, the way they beat him till his face was a bloody mess and he no longer groaned when the cowboy hit him. The one doing the hitting was a big strapping fellow with long arms that lashed out like whips, and every time he struck Chalk you could hear it, his knuckles smacking meat and bone.

Finally the two holding him turned him loose and he sank to his knees in the dirt, his blood splotching the ground with drops the size of half dollars. He lay there without moving. Waco nodded toward a man standing by a fire they heated their branding irons in and the fellow pulled one of the irons from the coals and brought it with him as the one who'd done the battering bent and ripped Chalk's shirt, exposing his back muscles and shoulder blades.

"Do it," Waco said to the brander.

Chalk jerked even though he was out cold when the brand burned into his flesh. The sound and smell was something I knew I'd never forget.

"Now break his hands," Waco said. The slugger went to a shed and came back with a hammer and smashed Chalk's hands with it. I flinched but didn't look away. I owed him at least that much—not to look away.

"Now get him the hell off my land," Waco said, giving me one last hard look. "And don't you or him ever come back here."

I dismounted and lifted Chalk and spilled him into the buggy, then tied my horse on back and climbed into the seat and took the reins and snapped them. It was all I could do to keep my hand off my gun.

I drove steady the rest of that day and through the night, stopping only when I needed to give the horses a blow. I washed canteen water over Chalk's face and checked his heartbeat. He'd come to then and would go under again. I did the best I could to keep him comfortable, but there wasn't much could be done. We finally reached the outskirts of Coffin Flats about the same time as dawn did. The streets were fairly well deserted, the town still asleep.

Chalk was by then shivering and muttering in his delirium, his face swollen terribly, blood crusted in the corners of his eyes and ears and nostrils. I kept seeing in my mind the way they beat him, smelled the burning of his flesh when they branded him. He held his broken hands out away from him like shattered birds.

Johnny Waco wanted to make sure that he was never out of Chalk Bronson's thoughts. I knew looking at the lawman, Johnny Waco was never going to be out of my thoughts either.

I pulled in at the hotel and went inside and found the kid there half asleep behind the desk.

"Where's there a doctor?"

He looked at me through lidded dull eyes.

"Doctor!" I said.

"Doc Flax has a place up the street above the druggist," he said. Then he realized I didn't know anything about the town and pointed. "That way."

I quickly drove there and pounded on the door at the top of the stairs but nobody answered. Went back again to the hotel. The kid was picking his nose and staring at his finger.

"Where's the marshal live?"

"Up that way," he said, pointing the opposite direction of the doctor's. "Little yeller house end of the street and over one—to your right."

So that's where I went.

I pounded on the door till a woman answered. She was wearing a checked robe and her face was puffy with sleep.

"You Mrs. Bronson?"

"Yes," she said.

"Help me get your husband out of the buggy."

Together we got him in the house and onto a bed. She was distressed, asking me over and over again what had happened. I told her we needed to get a doctor and did she know where he lived and she said yes and I told her to direct me and she did. I went and found the medico and he hurried back with me his shirttail hanging out, and when he saw Chalk he said, "Good God!"

I stood out in the living room while they attended to him, and realized I'd not slept in the last twenty-four hours and the world seemed otherwise a shitty place to be. I went and stood out front and watched the soft falling rain that had started and quit and started again ever since the day before—rain like sorrow, like God's own tears—and wished I had a drink and a place to lay down. I paced then, thinking I ought to do something but not knowing what, if anything would make a difference.

Finally they came out, the doctor and the woman—Chalk's wife.

"He'll live," the doctor said. "But it will be some time before he's back to anything close to normal. His hands are all busted and I . . . well, I did the best I could for him." He looked at the wife.

Chalk's wife's eyes were red and teary. They saw I had blood on my clothes.

"Ma'am, if it wouldn't be any trouble, I could use a cup of coffee and a place to wash up."

They wanted to know what happened and I

told them—the part about the beating but not why, or delivering Antonia; that was a little more complicated, considering. I could see the strain on Chalk's wife as it was and figured why make it worse.

"Thank you for bringing him home," she said in a very soft voice. She was dark-haired and broad-faced with gray eyes—what you might call plain, but she had a sense of goodness about her, that deep-down kind of goodness you don't sense many people have. I thought about how different she was from Antonia, how they must have compared in Chalk's mind—the two of them, different as night and day on the surface, but maybe the same in ways a stranger like myself couldn't see.

Chalk's wife showed me where I could wash up and then poured me a cup of Arbuckle and I drank the coffee and said I was sorry I had to bring her husband home in that condition and I was sorry there was nothing I could do to prevent it. She wanted to know why anyone would do what they did to him and I said I didn't know because the truth wasn't in play just then. She wept, and I stood and said I needed to go but that I would stop back by and look in on her and Chalk. The doctor walked out with me and when we were outside he said, "What the hell is the story here?"

"It has to do with a woman," I said.

"Antonia," he said.

"Yeah."

"Goddamn it."

He looked back toward the house.

"I warned Chalk to stay away from her."

"It's not exactly like it sounds."

"I knew them from before," he said. "They were good together once, then it all went to shit and now look what's happened. Somebody ought to go out and shoot that Johnny Waco in his goddamn face. Chalk's a good man, maybe too good for his *own* good."

He tucked his shirt in and said, "Whatever your interests are here, you'd be wise to get on your nag and ride away."

"Shit, I'm already gone," I said.

He looked at me and I knew those eyes had seen a lot of bloody things but I don't know if they'd ever seen a man branded and his hands broken with a hammer.

He walked away shaking his head.

I just hoped Antonia remembered the plan and stuck to it.

Chapter Eight

I needed rest bad and I went to my hotel, and the old man, Raford, was behind the desk again still reading that same book about Don Quixote and grinning as he followed his finger underneath the sentences. He looked up when he saw me enter and stopped grinning.

"You tell Chalk Bronson I was John Wesley Hardin?" I said.

He shook his head.

"I've been known to kill men for less than lying."

The color drained out of his face.

I held my gaze on him then said, "Don't be running my business out on the streets, you hear me?"

He nodded.

I went up to my room and undressed and lay down on the bed and for once I didn't sleep like a dead man—only a half-dead man.

I woke and there was still a little light in the room coming through the window and I rose and got dressed and armed myself and carried my Henry downstairs. The old man was still there only he avoided my gaze. I went out and slipped the rifle into the scabbard of my horse and walked him down to the livery and told the man to feed and rub him down and I'd be back later for him.

I walked to the town's only restaurant and went in and it was full of diners and I had to stand by the door to wait for an empty table. Then the waitress came over and said, "The lady over in the corner wondered if you'd care to join her?" I looked and it was the prostitute, Lorri, Pink Huston's woman. She was looking twice as beautiful as the last time I saw her—and sober and without the cat.

I worked my way past tables and said, "Nice of you to offer."

She smiled up at me. "Well, a man has to eat, right?"

"Right."

I took off my hat and set it on the floor next to my chair opposite her.

"Where's your . . . what should I call him, Pink?"

"Whatever you like. The steaks here are wonderful," she said.

So that's what I ordered, a steak and a glass of beer. Lorri was eating a small round steak, cutting it into delicate pieces. Her eyes were large and wet looking. She looked like she was dressed for the opera, with a black beret decorated with small white beads, a white blouse with lace tatting and black bone buttons and ruffled cuffs. I couldn't see without being obvious exactly what sort of skirt or shoes she was wearing, but her fingers were bejeweled with a variety of rings, mostly silver with rubies and other precious stones. She looked like something you'd want to keep.

"So, how are you and Antonia getting along?" she said as I waited for my meal.

I shrugged, said, "Antonia?"

She sipped from her wineglass and tilted her head far enough back to make it seem she was looking down her nose at me.

"I know she went to meet you the other morning after you'd come to the hog farm," she said.

"What else do you know?"

She smiled coyly and cut herself another little piece of steak and chewed it in a way I've never seen a woman eat anything before.

"I know she hasn't come back to the hog farm and Pink's more than a little pissed he's lost one of his best girls."

"I thought you were his best girl?"

She stopped chewing.

"I'm my own woman," she said. "I'm with Pink because I choose to be with him, not the other way around."

"Seems like an odd pairing, you don't mind the observation," I said. "You and Pink."

"Call it convenient," she said.

"You can tell him Antonia probably isn't coming back," I said.

"And can I also tell him why that would be?"

"She's gone back to her husband Johnny Waco."

I watched her mull that one over as she took another sip of her wine.

"I guess I'm a little relieved," she said after she set her glass back down again. The waitress brought my steak and I dug in right away, my belly crawling with anticipation. She waited until I took a break.

"What?" I said, from the way she was looking at me.

"I thought maybe Antonia and you had taken up together. I never thought she'd ever go back to Johnny Waco."

"Me?"

She smiled.

"And if she had taken up with me, so what?"

"I'd be disappointed."

"Why is that?"

"I sort of thought about taking up with you myself," she said.

It was my turn to smile. "Yeah, I bet a dollar you did."

Her hand reached across the table and rested atop mine, the one I held the knife with.

"You'd lose if you did bet a dollar," she said.

"It's a tempting offer," I said. "But my dance card is sort of full right now, Lorri."

She removed her hand slowly.

"You don't find me attractive?"

"Quite the opposite."

"Then why not act it and ask me to leave with you right now and go back to your hotel room?"

"I'd like that," I said. "But I don't need trouble with Pink, and I've got something I have to do tonight."

"Funny," she said. "I never figured you for a man who would be afraid of Pink. Maybe I misjudged you, Mister . . . I guess I don't even know your name."

"Jim Glass," I said. "That's my name, and you can think whatever you want about me. It doesn't matter—not really."

I finished eating my steak and she watched me and it was damn tempting to just say to hell with it and take her back to my hotel room. But I kept seeing Chalk's battered face, those smashed and broken hands, the wounded look on Antonia's face when she was being ordered around by Johnny. I kept smelling the stink of flesh burnt by a branding iron.

I reached in my pocket and my fingers felt the fat envelope—half a thousand dollars. Riding money, or riding around money? It was something I needed to decide. But then again, I'd already decided.

I called for the bill—both bills—Lorri's and mine, and paid for both our meals and left a nice tip because I was either feeling magnanimous or suicidal.

"Jim . . ." she said.

"Maybe another time," I said.

"I won't count on it," she said.

I stood and adjusted my hat and looked at her one last time. She really was beautiful and I really was a goddamn fool.

I went out and it was still raining softly and the night sky had that red to it—that faded red that feels ominous. The rain pattered off my brim as I walked back down to the livery and had the man saddle my horse. I said, "I'd like to buy a spare horse from you and a saddle."

"I got one I could let go for forty dollars, saddle included."

He showed it to me, a smallish mare that seemed sound after I ran my hands over her. "Lace her up," I said.

I undid my bedroll and took out my slicker and put it on then tied things back together and mounted my horse and took the reins of the spare after paying the man.

"Piss poor night to go riding," he said.

"Don't remind me."

I rode over to Chalk's place and tied both horses off out front then stepped up under the overhang and shook off my hat before knocking on the door and waiting for Chalk's wife to answer.

She stepped aside to allow me entry.

"How's he doing?" I said.

"He's awake, but I just gave him a spoonful of laudanum."

"Maybe I should just go and see him later," I said.

"No, he said earlier if you came 'round he wanted to talk to you."

"Okay."

She opened the bedroom door for me and then closed it. He was on his back on the bed, his hands bandaged, and when she closed the door he turned his head and looked at me, the lamp's light glittering in his half-swollen eyes.

I pulled up a chair next to the bed. His voice was raspy when he asked me where things stood.

"I'm on my way back there now," I said.

"You saw what he did to me," he said. "He'll do worse to you if he catches you."

"Unless she changes her mind, I should be okay."

"Where will you go—the two of you?"

I shrugged. "Someplace far away from here. Better you don't know."

"I don't—" He coughed and you could see it hurt him to do that. "I don't know why you're doing this," he said. "The money," I said. "Why else?"

"You could just let it go . . . long as she stays with him, he won't do anything to this town . . ."

"Yeah, I could, couldn't I?"

His eyes shifted behind the swollen lids. They went from my eyes to his ruined hands then back again.

"I made her a promise," I said. "I took your money so I guess I made you a promise too."

"You see what it cost me . . ."

"Yeah. I'm sorry I didn't do anything."

He shook his head. "He'd have killed you."

"Some things can be worse than dying."

"No," he said. "They can't . ."

The door opened again and his wife said, "Chalk, are you needing anything, honey?"

He shook his head.

I stood away from the bed.

"I was just leaving, ma'am."

She seemed relieved. She walked to the front door with me.

"There's more going on here than you're telling me," she said.

"No ma'am."

"I'm not so young and naive I don't know when a man is lying to me, Mr. Glass."

"No ma'am, I didn't reckon you were."

"Please don't come back around here anymore."

"Yes ma'am."

She closed the door, and it was just me and the two horses and the rain outside and a long road back to a dangerous place.

I saddled up and took the reins of the spare and headed back to Johnny Waco's spread. I had the little map Antonia had drawn for me there in the hotel room when she agreed to my plan —the map to where she would meet me. I had to get there by tomorrow night—to the grove of trees she'd drawn on the paper, by a stream a mile from the main house.

"It's the only place I can hide for a short time," she'd said. "I'll wait until Johnny's asleep and sneak out—let's say midnight—and wait for you there. But if you're not there by one in the morning, I'll have to go back or he'll send his drovers for me. Bring a horse. A good fast horse."

Words wrote on paper but like words branded on skin, far as I was concerned. I figured to ride steady till daylight and beyond, stop and rest till it got dark then make my way in the night to the grove and be there waiting for her. After that I thought we'd figure out together where to go—Texas, maybe.

The rain let up and pretty soon the moon broke between clouds that looked like black silver in the night sky and helped light the road ahead of us like it was something meant to be.

I could have spent the hours thinking of all the things that could go wrong, but what was the point? Either things would go right or they wouldn't. Either I'd live to someday tell the story or I wouldn't. The way I looked at most of

101

life was that in a hundred years nobody would care what you did or didn't do. The only thing that mattered was what you knew for yourself you did or didn't do.

This felt like the right thing to do.

It was a little like what the late Mr. Lincoln said about religion: "When I do right I feel right, and when I do bad I feel bad, and that is my religion."

I guess it was my religion too.

CHAPTER NINE

When the stranger offered her salvation, she took it. For enslaved she was and enslaved she knew she would forever be. But she'd rather be enslaved to her vices than to a man like Johnny Waco. She would rather be dead than to be enslaved to Johnny Waco. So she'd taken the man's offer, that he would come for her and that he would take her to a place called refuge. All she had to do was say she wanted it. And so she'd said it, hopeless as it might seem.

She craved the dragon more than she craved life. But the dragon would not come as long as she was in the clutches of Johnny Waco. He would have Maria tie her to her bed, as he had done before. And she would wretch up her insides and her head would hurt until she was nearly blind from the pain. Maria would force cold soup down her and call her privately a *puta* in disdain and stare at her with eyes as cold and calculating as a snake.

She suspected Maria of being Johnny's *puta,* of wanting to replace her as his wife. She cared not for Pedro, her dark, slump-shouldered and meek husband. She treated him cruelly and ignored his efforts and criticized him in front of Johnny.

She'd heard Maria whispering one time—the two of them, Johnny and she—and noticed the way Maria's demeanor softened whenever Johnny was near. She was openly flirtatious, even when Pedro was there; especially when Pedro was there. She flaunted her heavy breasts in low-cut blouses, the weight and shape of them like large loose fruit.

She was surprised that Maria did not slap her face when she was ill from the sobering effects.

So she tried to escape down the dark tunnel of her dope-filled dreams, escape reality for a different reality. She knew that if she did not try and leave, she would end up dying in the household of Johnny Waco. He would kill her slowly and indirectly.

In fact he had said to her not long after her secret bloody visit to Dr. Flax, "Was it mine, the child you lost?"

Dr. Flax had betrayed her no differently than she had been betrayed by any other man.

"No," she said. "It wasn't yours."

"Then I'm glad you lost it."

At that moment she knew she could not feel any more hate for anyone than what she felt for Johnny.

"I'm glad I lost it too," she said.

He slapped her hard across the face. It was nothing compared to the pain she'd already felt.

"Hit me again."

He hit her again, with his open hand. The sound of it was like someone letting a screen door slam shut.

The taste of her own blood gave her a private satisfaction. Would that he crucify her and make the act complete. Would that he shoot her, she could not have wanted more from him.

Instead he called Maria and told her, "Take care of my wife!"

"Si, señor, Johnny."

That bit of familiarity that had become so common, shared between them. She saw the looks the two of them exchanged and was sure of her suspicions.

Now she'd gone back to him again, at the request of the stranger.

She was already making plans.

If he failed her, well, what surprise was there

in that? She had her own plan. She did not trust completely even the stranger, but there was one man she felt she could trust, and she had summoned him earlier that day of her planned escape.

"Pedro," she said. He was standing in the shade of the house, smoking a cigarette. Maria was somewhere in the kitchen preparing supper at the opposite end of the long house.

He looked up at her, his eyes sorrowful from what she guessed was long years of marital misery. His rough straw hat was broken in places.

"Si, señora."

"I want to ask you a favor."

She took the money and put it in his hand.

"I want you to do me a favor you cannot speak of to Maria or Señor Waco . . ."

He looked at the money. It was a lot of money.

"It is not necessary," he said, handing it back, but she refused to take it. "The money isn't only for the favor," she said. And when he continued to look baleful, she said, "It's for everything you've done until this moment. Do you understand?"

He nodded. "Yes, I understand," he said.

She wanted him to get her a gun from Johnny's cabinet and bring it to her unseen.

He demurred at first.

"Will you do it?"

"Yes. But I don't want your money . . ."

"No. You keep it. You don't have to say anything to Maria about the money either." His gaze revealed nothing, whether or not he'd do it, whether he'd tell Maria, whether he'd tell Señor Johnny, his boss. Pedro was inscrutable.

"Something small," she said. "And loaded."

CHAPTER TEN

I made steady time, and after what seemed forever dawn broke over the prairies bright and clean as a new penny. I knew from what Chalk had told me before that I was well onto Johnny Waco's spread and I'd need to keep an eye peeled for any of his hands. Here and there windmills clattered and shifted around in the uncertain morning wind pumping up groundwater that spilled from lead pipes into water tanks. I took advantage of them to water the horses and wash my face and neck, and to try and awaken my weary senses.

I climbed one of the wood towers to get my bearings, and way off in the distance I could see the tin roofs of the buildings gleaming. I swung my gaze wide of them, following the directions on Antonia's hand-drawn map until I spotted the grove of trees—like the bristles on a paintbrush now that the leaves had shed off them. Then I climbed down and looked for a likely spot to hole up till nightfall.

There's something consoling about the sound of the blades of a windmill clacking in the wind.

I rode off in the general direction of the grove, taking my time, looking for a lay-up. I finally spotted an old line shack with the windows all busted out and the door missing and chose it.

Tired as I was I knew I had to be on my guard for any of Waco's men. I led the horses inside with apologies to them then settled down for the long day to unwind.

Wind blew through the open spaces—the windows and door and holes in the rotted roof—and I spent some time reading the old catalogue pages whichever old boys who had lived there before had tacked up over the years. I wondered where those old punchers were today, what they'd seen and how many of them died as broke as the day they were born and how many had married and how many of them came to bad ends or ended up preachers or store clerks or outlaws or lawmen.

Thing with old buildings is they got a history same as any man—the history of all who lived in them—the weddings and funerals that took place in them, the love and hate that hid between their walls, and that was something that always interested me, the history of buildings.

The horses snorted their restlessness and I

talked to them, some in Spanish, the little bit I'd learned down in Texas, calling them sweetheart and just making up things to talk to them about. And before I knew it my thoughts turned to Fannie and our time spent there on that prairie grass together where the fenceline ran true as God's finger, the wire glazed by the sun, and I couldn't help but smile even in light of the heartbreak she caused me, because no matter how bad those things turn out—and they always turn out bad—your mind just naturally remembers the good parts. And in spite of nothing what we shared being true, I still considered myself a lucky man to have been part of it. Anytime a beautiful woman gives herself to you, consider yourself lucky.

Clouds passed before the sun, creating great shadows over the grass—dark shapes moving like something alive—and it made for a pretty sight.

Then I heard the whicker of horses and all that pleasant mood changed in a heartbeat.

Two riders topped a slight rise and sat surveying the lay of things. One looped his leg 'round his saddle horn and fumbled in his coat pocket till he came out with makings and rolled himself a shuck. They were both wearing bat-wing chaps and I could see they had rifles in their scabbards. They sat there for a time, the wind carrying smoke from the one's cigarette. One of their horses whickered and then one of mine answered. The riders both turned and looked toward the line shack.

A piece of bad luck on my part if they decided to ride down and take a look.

They did.

I drew my revolver because I sure as shit didn't want to have to shoot those old boys with my rifle, which I easily could have. I didn't want to shoot them at all, but if I did shoot them it would be because they wouldn't leave me any choice, and it would have to be close-in work.

They rode down the slope cautious, looking for where the sound of the horse had come from. It was that little racer I'd bought off the liveryman.

They got close then circled the shack, never suspecting a horse would be inside with another horse and a man holding a pistol.

"Where you think it come from?" one of them said.

"Hell if I can make it out, down from around here somewhere."

"I don't see no horse, do you?"

"I don't see no horse neither."

"I heard it said they's ghost horses in this country."

"I ain't never heard nothing like that. What the hell's a ghost horse anyways?"

"I guess it's just some old horse or something, I don't know. It was a Indian told me."

"Indian?"

"Pawnee Indian."

"Listen."

"What is it?"

They stopped circling the shack.

I stepped out behind them with the Merwin Hulbert cocked and aimed.

"You boys step down from those horses."

They looked 'round slow.

"Don't make me shoot you all."

One was young, the other quite a bit older.

The older one said, "Why you want to shoot us?"

"Because you all might ride back and get some others and come back here and shoot me."

The younger one said, "Shit, that don't hardly make no sense."

"Yeah, it does," the older one said. "That's the fellow was with Chalk Bronson the other day."

"This isn't a debate," I said. "Get off those mounts. And do it cautious; I've not had my coffee yet and my hands are a little shaky, and I've got the pull on this trigger set light anyway so it wouldn't take much—might even just go off by itself."

They stepped down holding their reins.

"What you all doing back here?" the older one said. He had iron gray moustaches—an old boot who wasn't ever going to do anything but run cows and ride fence and work for men like Waco. "You got some sort of death wish?" he asked.

"Take that rope, junior, and tie your partner up," I said to the younger one.

He looked sheepish.

"I'll shoot you in the knees," I said. "Do it."

He unhooked his rope and wrapped it around the old man, and I said, "Truss him up good, like a mossy horn steer."

He said, "I'm sorry, Bob."

And the old man said, "Don't you worry none about it, I know it ain't nothing personal you got against me, Torrence."

When he got old Bob trussed up, I said, "Sit down on the ground." And when he stood defiant, I went and shoved him down and told the kid to lay facedown next to Bob, and he did and I took Bob's rope and trussed the kid up good.

"Now what?" Bob said.

"Now nothing," I said.

"Well ain't this the shits."

"I reckon maybe it is."

I hauled them one by one inside the shack and set them up against the wall and said, "Once I get my business done here, I'll let some of your pals know where you are if you ain't worked yourself loose from those ropes."

"They's wolves all over this country," the younger one said. "And snakes."

"Too cold for snakes and I'll bet there's not been a wolf seen in these parts for ten years," I said. "I don't guess you have to worry about nothing but me."

"We all just gone sit here till what?" the old man said. "I got to take a piss. Piss all the time here lately—ever' hour or so. Then when I try it takes me a while to get started and a while to stop. Goddamn but it ain't like my life ain't miserable enough, now I got to run into you."

"I sure as hell am sorry about your problems, Bob. You give me your word you won't try anything stupid and I'll untie you."

"You got my word. I spent all my stupid letting you catch me once."

I untied him and walked outside with him and watched as he went and stood off with his back to me and fumbled at his front and stood there with his back arched trying to relieve himself.

I could hear him groaning. I felt bad in a way, because I knew we all get there someday—old like that with our plumbing messed up and our dignity gone but there wasn't nothing any of us could do about it—and I hoped when it came my time somebody would show me a little respect.

We probably stood there ten minutes before Bob finished up his business and I walked him back inside. I trussed him up again and he set down on his own accord next to his companion.

"How many men has Waco got working for him?" I said.

"All told? Maybe fifty," he said.

"They all stay close to the main house?" I said.

The old man raised his tied hands and knuckled back his hat. He had a grizzle of growth on a face looked like scrub growing out of dry land cut by rain and wind.

"Nah, they're scattered all over this here land."

"You aim to kill us, mister?" the younger one said.

"No, he ain't aiming to kill us, Torrence," Bob said. "He was aiming to do that, he'd already of done it."

They both looked at me.

"He's right," I said. "Bob is."

They sat there with their legs crossed at their boots. We all waited for nightfall.

It come dark and I led the horses outside after telling the two they best just keep quiet and let me go and do what I come here for, and Bob said, "What'd you come here for?"

"I come for the girl," I said. "And if you two follow me, help the others to follow me, and I get the chance, I'll shoot you both, just so you know."

Bob shook his head, said, "I'm a puncher not some man killer. Torrence ain't either."

Torrence shook his head too.

"Well, then, you all take care. I fixed those ropes so you all should work free of them shortly enough."

Outside, I spanked their horses with my hat, slapping them hard two or three quick times till they run off, knowing they wouldn't run off all that far but far enough to take those boys a while to catch up to them. Then I mounted up and rode off toward the grove.

It took me about an hour to make my way to the trees, and I could see them against the night sky standing stiff and dark and went up toward them figuring if she was there she'd recognize me.

She did, and stepped out.

I handed her the reins to the racer and she mounted up. She had a satchel and said it was spare clothes, and I said we ought to get moving and rode away toward the south, away from the main ranch buildings.

"How will we make our way?" she said, and I pointed up toward the sky.

"Stars," I said. "We'll navigate like sailors do."

"That what you were once, a sailor?" she said.

"No, but it don't mean I can't read stars."

We kept moving till sunup then stopped, rested the horses and let them graze a bit.

"I figure we can make the border to Texas in two, three days," I said.

She was dressed in man's clothing, rough coat, britches, low-heeled boots, and a felt hat with her hair tucked up under it. I watched her throat when she drank from the canteen. It was a nice delicate throat.

I stood watching the direction we'd come from to see if we were being pursued. It was flat where we were now and you could see a pretty good distance. We'd left the main road earlier and cut overland but the grass, tall and dry as it was, left a clear trail for even a half-assed tracker.

I didn't see anything. Not yet, at least.

"How you holding up?" I said.

"I could use something for my head," she said.

"Maybe this would be a good time to consider getting off the booze and dope," I said.

"Yes, thank you for your advice," she said sarcastically.

"Just meant a clear head might be of some advantage when you're being chased by a man like Johnny Waco."

She looked too at the direction we'd just come from.

Except for the whisper of the wind over the brittle grass there didn't seem to be anything alive except her and I.

I shrugged and said, "Maybe he's not going to come after you . . ."

She laughed a short hard laugh.

"He'll be coming," she said.

"Maybe not. Maybe he figures you keep running away, what's the point. Maybe he'll just find himself another woman—one who will stay home."

She tightened the cinch on her saddle like a woman who knew a lot about such things, then mounted.

"He's coming," she said and patted the satchel.

"What's in there besides some of your underthings?"

She smiled. "Enough of his money to last me a very long time."

"The five hundred wasn't enough for you?"

"It's not a matter of how much," she said, "but whose."

"So you robbed him?"

"Blind as a bat."

I looked back again and saw the column of dust from the road about the point we left it and cut across country.

"Yeah, he's coming," I said.

And we rode like hell.

CHAPTER ELEVEN

We stayed ahead of them as though we were out-racing our own shadows, and at one point Antonia came alongside me and shouted, "Follow me!" and I did without hesitation. I saw the town rise out of the grass and heard a train whistle blowing.

We were practically off our horses before we fully had them stopped, the train just pulling away from the station. I helped lift her aboard one of the cars then ran to catch up and finally got aboard just as the train picked up speed. You could smell the steam off its engine, the hot cinder along the track.

We found seats in one of the cars and sat across from each other and in a little while the train conductor came down the aisle asking for tickets. When he reached us I said we didn't have any tickets and could we buy some from him.

"Where you headed?" he said.

"Where does this train go?"

"All the way to Refugio."

"We'll take two tickets to Refugio, then," I said. "How much?"

He was a short thick-set man in his middle

years wearing a black cap and coat and his shoes were polished. A silver watch chain with a fob hung from his waistcoat buttonhole to the pocket.

"It's not policy to purchase tickets onboard," he said. "I'll have to put you off at the next stop and you'll have to pay the ticket master there."

"Look," I said, taking the envelope from my pocket with the city council money in it. I peeled off fifty dollars and held it out to him. "Do you think that will cover it—the fare?"

"Mister, that's way too much."

"You got a private car for rent on this line?"

He nodded.

"Would that cover the trip and a private car and your troubles?"

"Yes sir, it would."

"Then if you wouldn't mind."

He led us back up the aisle and into another car and through that one into a third that had private rooms on one side. He opened the door to one of them and let us in and told us that the dining car was one car back and lunch would be served—he pulled out his watch, the one hooked to the silver chain, and looked at it—in half an hour. I thanked him and closed the door.

Antonia had taken off her hat and set it on the velvet-covered seat beside her. Her hair tumbled down to her shoulders, a nice dark brown thicket. She unbuttoned her coat and I could see the free weight of her breasts inside the peasant shirt, the V of it held loosely together with a thick string. She didn't have those sleepy doped eyes now. They were alert and alive with excitement or whatever it was she was feeling after the chase. I sat down opposite her and took my own hat off and ran my fingers through hair that needed a cut and had shagged over the back of my collar. I felt the stubble on my jaw as well and realized I probably smelled like horse sweat but knew this wasn't any time for worrying about formalities. She smelled like a cake of soap, what I smelled of her.

She still held the valise on her lap, gripping the handle with both hands.

"Did you take it because you wanted to make sure he'd come after you?" I said, thinking it was a damn dumb thing of her to do if she really wanted to be free of the guy.

"He owes me this much and more," she said. "But it's not that."

"Then what is it?"

"I just wanted to take something from him I knew he cared about—like he took from me."

I looked out the window, the prairie slipping past in a hurry, the telegraph poles like tall straight lines, the train's own squat shadow just down below. I could feel the vibration up through the soles of my boots.

"Once we hit Refugio you feel safe enough to strike out on your own?"

"Yes."

"Then that's what we'll do."

"What about you?" she said. "Where will you go?"

"Better neither of us knows where the other is headed."

"Why? I mean we pulled it off."

"I doubt a man like Waco will quit that easy. And if either of us is caught we can't say about the fate of the other if we don't know."

"You'd tell if he caught you?"

"I might. You might too. I saw what he did to Chalk Bronson for some perceived slight."

Her light demeanor changed just then.

"What do you mean?" she said.

"You were there."

"No, I went inside, remember."

"You weren't curious?"

"No. I mean I didn't want to know, I suppose."

"He broke his hands," I said. "He branded him and broke his hands after he had him beaten by a couple of his cowboys."

She turned her face away and I could see she was fighting back tears.

"You still love him?"

"Who, Johnny? I never loved Johnny."

"No, I mean Chalk."

She wiped at her wet eyes with the heel of her hand.

"No."

"I think he does you, a little, as much as loving two women at the same time allows him to."

She looked at me then again, fiercely, intently.

"Once it's gone, it's gone," she said. "Love is."

"I wouldn't know," I said. "I only come close to it one time, and not all that close."

"It hurts to the same degree it feels good."

Then we seemed to run out of words and after a little while she lay down across her seat using the satchel as a pillow and I said I was going to walk out on one of the platforms and have a smoke. She closed her eyes. I didn't smoke, but used it as an excuse to go and have a drink in the dining car alone. The last thing I needed was for her to get drunk.

I found an empty table and a black porter came over wearing a white shirt and black trousers and said, "Suh, we don't serve nothin' to eat for 'nother half an hour."

"Can I get a whiskey?"

"Yas suh."

He went off and returned in a few moments with a whiskey and I paid him for it and sat there looking out the window and taking my time with it. In spite of everything, it seemed like high adventure to me—having a runaway wife of a real bad guy and a satchel full of his stolen money. And to think I could be clerking in some general store somewhere, selling notions to fat ladies in big hats. I asked the porter to bring me another whiskey when he came to get the glass and asked him when we were scheduled to pull into Refugio and he said around ten o'clock that evening.

I figured when we got there, I'd send a telegram to Chalk letting him know the plan had been successful, if nothing else to give him the satisfaction that Waco no longer had possession of Antonia. Small comfort, I'm sure, but comfort nonetheless I guessed.

I finished the second drink—not as good as the first, because the first of anything is always better than what comes after it—and walked back to the car. She was sitting in the corner of the couch, her feet and bare legs tucked up underneath her, her trousers and boots lying on the floor. She held a silver flask in her right hand and I could see whatever she was drinking was already starting to take its effect, for her face was flushed and her eyes dreamy.

"What the hell is that?" I said.

"Absinthe," she said, holding it to me. "Have some."

"No. I know all about it."

She smiled warmly.

The valise was open next to her and I could

see lots of loose money in it—so much so it didn't even seem real.

"Tell me about the women you never loved but almost did," she said.

The sky outside was gray again and little drops of rain streaked the car window even as the world seemed to be moving one way and we another. The two whiskeys I'd had were just enough to make me reconsider her—the wan and almost vulnerable creature, half naked, all that money, daring me to play the game.

I sat down across from her.

"Is that what you really want to do, talk about the women I almost loved but never did?"

"Or something like it," she said.

She leaned over and placed the hand holding the flask in my lap and let it rest there.

"Are you sure you won't have some?" What I saw in her gaze was the promise of all things.

Everything about it was wrong. But then temptation always has a wrongness to it. We ended up falling asleep pressed together but that was all, the rhythm of the train stealing our resistance to sleep—stealing it like money.

We awoke to the rapping of our door, the conductor calling, "Refugio ten minutes!"

I fumbled around in the dark for my boots, found a match and struck it to the small lantern above the couch. I tried not to stare at her while she dressed. The feelings I had were the same feelings I had when I found out Fannie had been keeping time with me and Junior Bosch at the same time. Only instead of Junior doing it to me, it felt like it was something I was doing to Chalk Bronson, coveting his woman, the woman he entrusted me to save, even though by all accounts she wasn't his woman at all. She was legally Johnny Waco's woman and I didn't know *how* I felt about that part.

"What will you do when we get off the train?" I said.

"I thought we weren't going to tell each other."

"That was about where we'd go once we hit Refugio."

"I don't know what I'll do," she said. "Possibly see my father again."

"He a good man, your father?"

"Yes."

"Mother?"

"Dead," she said. "Long time."

"Brothers or sisters?"

She shook her head.

"Five minutes to go in our coexistence," she said, "and we're having a real conversation. That usually comes before what we did."

"I apologize."

"For what?"

"It felt like I wanted to take advantage of you, Antonia."

"Maybe you should have."

I offered her my best leer. "Another time and place, different circumstances, who knows."

"Yes," she said. "Who knows . . ."

We felt the train slowing and then at one point it lurched ahead after we'd thought it stopped and it threw us together and we held each other not knowing if the damn train had finally stopped or not or if we should unhand each other or what.

Finally we did.

"Good luck," she said as we stepped off the train into a cloud of steam, the night dark around us except for the lights of the town up ahead.

"You too," I said.

What we didn't know was there was only one hotel in town and we both ended up taking rooms there—but not together.

"You hungry?" I said as we climbed the stairs.

"Yes, you?"

"Starved."

"I guess taking a meal together wouldn't commit us to anything."

"Don't see how it would."

"You buying?" she said after we'd set our things in our rooms and locked the doors and gone down to the dining room and been given seats.

"You are," I said. "I paid for the train tickets, remember."

She smiled and we ordered steaks and I could still see that dreamy doped look in her eyes and wished it wasn't there, but it was what it was and there was nothing I could do about it except maybe privately grieve that a woman with such potential wanted to waste herself.

We ate slowly and I asked her to tell me more about herself.

She shrugged. "What is there to tell, really?"

"How did you end up with Johnny Waco, for instance? He seems the complete opposite of Chalk Bronson."

"Long story, but the short of it is, I thought Chalk had been killed in the war. I waited a long time without hearing anything from him and finally gave up hope that I ever would. The selection of men wasn't much as you can imagine in a place like Coffin Flats. Johnny had a big-time reputation of being a powerful man and at first he was charming as hell. You probably don't know it, but most of the real bastards can be charming as hell when they want to be." The look she gave me didn't fail to register.

"Yeah, some gunfighters are like that too."

She smiled again and sipped the last of the wine in her glass and waited for me to refill it for her and I did, reluctantly.

"You're pretty charming yourself when you want to be," she said.

"You think so?"

"You see, that right there, that boyish innocence you sometimes put on."

"Well, it's worked in the past a time or two, I won't deny it."

"Me, I like to deal straight off the top of the deck, Mr. Glass."

"You sure know how to take the starch out of a man."

Her laugh was short, sharp, as she lifted her wineglass.

"To scoundrels and women like me," she said.

And when I didn't toast, she smiled and drank half the glass.

She went on to tell me about her father, an attorney for the railroad at one time who'd made a lot of money through wise investments and was now semiretired. She said his name was Dalton Stone and that he lived in Denver where he took on cases he mostly couldn't win but ones he believed innocent men had been convicted of crimes they didn't commit or where there was a real sense of injustice. I thought it interesting.

"How did you meet Chalk?" I said.

She smiled warmly, the candlelight infusing her eyes.

"Him," she said. "He was part of a medicine show that came to Denver when I was nineteen. Doc Rainey's Patent Medicine Wagon. Chalk was driver and helper to Doc Rainey. They even had an Indian princess who claimed she'd been healed from crippling diseases . . ." She shook her head, remembering. "Chalk was dressed in a bright blue bib shirt with white buttons and a pair of woolly chaps." She clapped her hands happily. "God, he had a hat on big enough to block out the sun. But he was so handsome I couldn't take my eyes off him. And after the show my father took me to meet Doc Rainey—who also performed magic tricks. Chalk was there by Doc's wagon lounging around spinning a rope."

She sighed and took another sip of her wine.

"He was young and handsome and shy as a colt and that's what attracted me to him. I went back to the show the next day alone and made it a point that we meet."

"A case of love at first sight?" I said.

"Yes, exactly. We'd decided to elope, have a preacher marry us and go off to Niagara Falls for our honeymoon. I knew my father wouldn't be happy, even though he'd come to like Chalk quite well . . ."

"It must have hurt when he went off to the war and didn't come back."

"Like you can't even imagine. I met Johnny and thought I could be happy again, but all I was was miserable and eventually I started doing this stuff." She held up the wine. "Then a friend introduced me to cocaine pills—washing them down with whiskey. It took some of the heartache away—quite a bit of it. I discovered the pleasures of opium after . . ."

"Hooking up with Pink," I said.

The pleasantness of her face changed to something other.

"I didn't mean to pry," I said.

"Yes, you did."

"Not to dredge up hurtful things."

"I want to write Chalk a letter. One last letter to let him know I'm sorry for all that's happened to us. Do you think that would be all right?"

"Don't see what it could hurt."

"I wish I could go back and change everything to the way it was," she said.

"We all do—sooner or later."

We finished dinner and went up the stairs together and I walked her to her door and she paused for a moment as though wanting to say something, but then put the key in the lock and said only, "Good night."

I walked down to my room and did the same thing.

I kept telling myself I shouldn't be thinking what I was thinking.

The last thing on my mind was Johnny Waco and his bunch.

It should have been the first thing.

CHAPTER TWELVE

Morning light had filled the room and I was sitting on the side of the bed rubbing the sleep out of my eyes when the door caved in. Three men, two of them with shotguns aimed at me, suddenly made it crowded. The shorter one with the sugarloaf hat, holding only a short black revolver, said, "If you reach for that hog-leg there won't be enough left of you to put in a cigar box." My Merwin Hulbert resting in my holster that hung from the bed frame above my pillow looked a mile away.

Then he turned over the lapel of his coat to show me the badge.

"Sheriff Joe Bike," he said. "You're under arrest."

"For what?"

He looked at me as if I'd just asked if his mama was still a virgin.

"How about wife stealing? We take that shit 'round here fairly serious, mister."

I could hear voices out in the hall, one of them Antonia's: "Turn me loose you dirty bastard!"

I started to rise off the bed.

"I'd move real fucking slow I was you," the

lawman said. "These boys are the nervous types, seeing how they're new on the job."

I looked from the one to the other. They did indeed look nervous.

"Got her, boss," a fourth man said from out in the hallway, and Sheriff Bike turned his head to have a look then turned his attention back to me.

"Well, at least you got good taste," he said. "Take her on down to the jail, Tobe." Then to me, "Get dressed."

Twenty minutes later I was sitting in the man's jail, such as it was. I could hear Antonia cursing our captors in another room.

"Let me go, you son of a bitches."

"Holding you till they come get you, woman. You might as well shut that foul mouth of yours."

She continued to curse them and they continued to try and settle her down. This went on for nearly an hour.

Finally Sheriff Bike came back to where I was—a small eight-by-eight-foot (I measured by stepping it off) cell with naught but an iron cot.

"Real she-cat Johnny got himself," he said.

"You know Johnny Waco?" I said.

He looked at me with cornflower blue eyes you'd expect to see on a woman.

"He's my cousin," he said.

"How'd you track us down?"

"Telegraph, son. You heard of the telegraph, ain't you?"

"Yes, but how'd he know we were coming here?"

"Easy enough. That flyer you all took out of Coffin Flats—there's only one town between here and there worth even getting off at. Guess which one? You're in it."

"You know anything at all about your cousin?"

"Know he's rich and is generous to those who lend him a hand."

"He'll kill her if you send her back."

He looked toward the door and the room beyond it, where I'd heard Antonia's voice.

"True love," he said. "Never does run smooth, they say. It ain't my place to get into a man's marital affairs. It ain't yours neither."

"I was just trying to do her a favor. Trying to save her life. Seems to me that should be the job of the law, not the other way around."

"Real philosopher, ain't you?"

He turned and went out again, slamming the door closed behind him, shifting the bolt.

I waited all day for nothing to happen. Every so often I could hear Antonia laying into whoever it was and the one male voice said, "Now ma'am, there ain't no use to talk to me like this. I'm a Christian. There ain't no use to you abusing me so . . ."

Time dragged mercilessly.

Finally, sometime very late in the day, I heard new voices. Male voices. A shuffling of boots on wood, a door clanging open, Antonia's voice, then a slap then nothing. More doors closing again then silence.

An hour or so more and the door to where my cell was opened and dull light fell in and Sheriff Bike came in with two of his men.

"Well, she's on her way back home to her worried husband, exactly where a woman ought to be," he said. "Lucky thing for you is, Johnny don't want to press charges."

I waited for him to open the door and let me go, but knew it wasn't going to be that simple.

He nodded and one of the deputies stepped forward and then Bike opened the door and said, "He's just goin' put these handcuffs on you. Don't give him no shit, now, hear."

"Why handcuffs if you're letting me go?" I said.

"Because we're gonna ride you out a little ways then turn you loose, make sure you don't come back here no more. You look like the dangerous type. It's a precaution."

"You don't have to worry about that," I said. "I've got no reason to come back here."

"No, you sure as hell ain't," he said. "We just gone make sure is all."

I had a bad feeling—maybe the worst one I'd ever had.

"You try and fight this," he said, "I'm gonna shoot you in the head and say you tried to escape."

I let the kid deputy put the handcuffs on me.

"Now walk out the back there," Bike said.

They escorted me out the back door, where four saddle horses stood waiting. I was ordered to wait until two of them mounted their horses, and then Bike told me to do the same and then he mounted his too. Then one rode over to me and said, "Turn your head." And when I did he tied a kerchief over my eyes.

The air was chill and the wind tunneled down the alley where we were. The two riders in front led out. One of them had taken the reins and my horse followed. I could hear Bike behind me saying, "Let's take him to the meeting place, boys."

That bad feeling I had only got worse.

I tried to time in my mind how far we'd ridden or in which direction, but it was impossible. We rode for what seemed a goodly amount of time. I settled into the rhythm of life itself, figuring if they were going to kill me, there wasn't much I could do about it, and it sure seemed like that was exactly what they aimed to do take me somewhere out into the backcountry and kill me.

We rode along to the creaking of saddle leather, the jingle of bits, the clop of hooves against the hardpan.

Seemed at some point we rode down a slight incline and back up again after going through some water. Not long afterward Bike said, "Hold up here."

One rode up and took off my blindfold and I could see we were standing under a big spreading cottonwood, its leaves all but shed, its branches low. I figured it was a hanging tree.

"Get him down from there," Bike said, and they came and took me off my horse, my wrists still cuffed.

"This where you let me go, right?" I said, half mocking because I knew they'd not ridden me this far just to let me go.

"Something like that," Bike said and nodded at the two with him, who took hold of my arms. Bike made a show of it, pulling a pair of leather gloves he had hooked on his belt and putting them on.

"Hold him steady, boys," he said, then slammed his fist into my belly and almost as soon as it doubled me slammed another into my jaw and my world tipped over.

"You understand I'm doing this for your own good," he said. I tried to shake the ringing out of my ears. "So's you'll know there is always a penalty for doing wrong."

He hit me again and I think he broke a rib because it hurt like a son of a bitch, like something sharp going into my lung, and then hit me in the face again, his blow catching me just

135

above my right brow so that blood leaked into my eye. The guy knew what he was doing, snapping off the punch so it'd cut.

I almost went black from it and his voice seemed far away.

"Go bust a nice limb," I heard him say to one of them. They turned me loose and I dropped to my knees trying to wipe the blood out of my eye while trying to breathe. Bike stood there rubbing his hands together, looking at them like they were something he just discovered.

I heard a limb breaking, a splintering crack like a pistol shot.

"Stand him up and take off the cuffs," Bike said. They were like faithful dogs, those two. Once they had me uncuffed, they stretched my arms out to my sides and tied my wrists to the heavy thick limb they'd broken from the tree.

"Why hell," Bike said when they finished. "You look like Jesus—paying for your sins. Thou shall not covet thy neighbor's wife, ain't that right?"

I figured now was when they'd shoot me.

"You're free to go," Bike said, and I lifted my head as much as I could with the limb yoked to me and pressing into the back of my neck.

They mounted their horses and sat there looking down at me, the land falling to night all around, the stinging of my face, the blood from the cut above my eye drying to a crust.

"Don't come back to my town," Bike said.

"Don't ever let me see you again."

Then they turned and rode off and I watched them go before sinking to my knees. Every time I took a deep breath it felt like a knife going into my lungs. I worked my wrists but they'd been lashed to the limb with rawhide strips. I knew one thing: I couldn't allow myself to fall on my face or back or I'd never be able to rise again. Those old boys knew a thing or two about putting a man in a bad way. I forced myself up finally and realized that with night coming on fast I'd be a fool to try and make my way in the dark. I went over to the tree and placed my back against it and eased myself into a sitting position. With the support of the tree holding me up, I could at least sleep if I needed to, wait out the night, hope for better things in the morning. Where I was I couldn't say. I didn't see a road anywhere, no sort of trail.

With the night came a steady rain that soaked me through to the skin, and after a while I couldn't tell if what was flowing down my face was blood, rain, or tears.

And that money I'd done this for, well, they'd taken that too, back when they arrested me and put me in the jail. I was broke and yoked and abandoned, and with my luck running the way it was, I'd probably be dead in a few days.

Unless.

It was a big *unless*.

137

CHAPTER THIRTEEN

The metaphor, he told himself, was a boat adrift, its mooring rope cut, the water wide, turbulent, always astir. He was the rudderless boat guided by the unpredictable winds after her death. The winds were mighty, carrying him along with no real sense of purpose. The winds were nothing more than God's angry breath.

His name was Tom Twist. And somewhere in the distant past were the mountains and a grave on a plateau with her in it. It was as though God had come to visit and then simply stood suddenly and said goodbye and took her with Him.

He thought in metaphors these days. His heart had been assassinated. He had lived a good life for so long that now he felt the need to see the darker side. He bought a pair of fancy pistols off a man who said they once belonged to the famous but long dead Wild Bill, complete with matching holsters. Their weight felt right on his hips, balanced, deadly. He felt dangerous at last, a man to be feared.

He thought he could find solace in the sort of women men fought over and spent their last dollar on. The whorehouses of Cripple Creek and Silver City and all up and down the gold-fields offered him plenty of opportunity.

In every whore he searched for a little bit of his dead wife, the woman he had loved so hard and true. They disappointed, left him wanting, ashamed, sick. One girl came close; a small dark-haired twenty-year-old from Iowa. She said her name was Alice Blue and that she'd been raised on a farm and could still smell pig stink. He did not know how much of what she said was true. Every girl had a story of sorrow, every one had a certain sadness.

"My daddy would probably kill himself to know what I was doing now. Him and Mama were good Christian people."

The winter had set in. The gulches and hills were socked with wet fog, ice, snow. A dreary time to be a boat adrift. The mud came up to his knees.

Alice Blue had the laugh of a schoolgirl. She was young, naive, childish, and goodhearted—somewhere between a woman and a child, with budding breasts and thick legs. He could imagine her married someday with several children and having grown to fat.

He never told her who he was, what he'd been. He never told her about his dead wife, the life he'd lived. She never asked. She laughed and showed him her stockings, this well-fed Iowa farm girl. He liked that in her; it made her more wholesome than the others with their pocked faces and bad teeth and wasted bodies. But who could blame them for what they'd turned into? The men in those camps were the roughest there were. Hard as the rock they picked to get to the gold. They pried with dirty fingers the gold and the flesh with equal gusto, desire flaming in their brains. They also had rotted teeth and rotted breath from the rotted liquor and lack of personal hygiene. When they rose from the whores' beds, the sheets were filthy.

"Miners are terrible hard on a girl," she said.

She confessed to him many things about her life. She was as open as a book. And for a short while he was enchanted by her, thinking perhaps like God, love works in mysterious ways. And for a moment he allowed himself to believe that he *could* love her.

Then one day he awoke to discover her gone, and with her, his money. He suspected the man she called "cousin" was her pimp. He thought the price of his stolen poke fair wages for the sin. He did not try and find her, but let the wind fill him again, a boat without rudder or sail, the weight of wind mapping his path.

It didn't matter where he had been or where he was about to go, for he was in search of himself and nothing else. The self lost needed to be found again.

He came eventually into New Mexico and

saw the dark mesas long and flat and black against the evening sky—reaching forth like gigantic fingers of an outstretched hand. The sky at evening went from a soft pink to a deep rose before becoming like unpolished silver.

He came across the mouth of a cave one evening just after dusk, and from it flew thousands of bats and he sat and watched in amazement.

He had heard stories about New Mexico, about shape shifters and men who could turn themselves into animals, about the haunted grounds of the Hopi and the sacred grounds of the Navajo.

He knew a young priest who had gone and lived there and come back completely changed and married a woman and had children with her, believing, he said, that God did not want man to suffer alone, but to have himself children and a woman to love. The priest said, with tears in his eyes, that God *was* love and to deny love was to deny God.

Tom Twist heard the echoes of his horse's hooves within the canyon walls and upon loose rock.

The stars seemed closer than ever as he waited for sleep.

He was sure he had come to the right place. He was sure that whatever force was guiding him had led him to this place for a particular reason.

And then one day he saw what looked like a crucified man staggering alone, his arms spread outward, tied to a tree limb, and with the failing light it seemed to Tom that he was having a dream—for how could it be, the thing he was seeing?

And for a moment he held his breath thinking he was having a vision.

But then he saw the man fall and not get up.

He knew then there was a reason it was he who had come across this man and not someone else. But what that reason was, he could not yet say.

He rode forth.

CHAPTER FOURTEEN

That son of a bitch Joe Bike was right about one thing—after two days I was beginning to feel death chasing me. I was cold and miserable and half out of my head. When I found water to drink, I'd have to kneel and balance myself, leaning forward so I didn't fall flat on my face and end up helpless as a turtle on its back. The rain hammered me on and off through that first night and into the next and the day after that. The wind lashed across my face, at times making the rain feel like thorns, and my eye had swollen shut from the blow Bike struck me so that I had to turn my head to look at what was on my right. Making everything worse, more intense, was my broken rib, just trying to breathe. Every step was painful, but kneeling and rising again was excruciating. And every step I took stabbed more anger in me toward the men who did this to me, and especially the one who ordered it done: Johnny Waco.

At one point near the end of the second day I nearly lost my balance and fell flat and had to retch because my stomach was turning over with probably bad water I'd drank out of a dirty puddle. That night I found a stump of a tree to sit against and the dreams came bad and repeated themselves over and over and I kept waking every few minutes, shivering, my teeth chattering, the pain so great I wanted to scream and did.

The third day broke clean, or maybe it was the fourth, I'd lost track of time, and the sun offered some of its early winter warmth. But by then I might have even been walking in circles. At one point I looked up and saw buzzards wheeling in the sky and wondered if they had found something already dead, or were just waiting.

I knew no matter what, I had to keep moving. Every time I stopped and rested it was harder to get up again. At one point I spotted a cairn of rocks someone had stacked up and figured I'd give it one shot—to throw myself backward on those rocks and try and crack the limb I was lashed to.

I knew the chances of success were not great, that if I broke anything it would probably be one of my arms in trying. But I was desperate and a desperate man will do desperate things when he feels his luck is about run out.

I tried to think of the best way to do it and couldn't come up with a very good plan. So I just stood with my back to the rocks and then flung myself backward as hard as I could.

The pain nearly caused me to pass out.

I lay there trying to get my breath, the plan a complete failure, my hands scraped and cut, my back bruised and aching. I cursed. I wept. I bargained with God. Nothing seemed to help.

It took every last bit of my strength and three tries but I finally managed to lift myself up again.

I staggered on. Toward what, I didn't know. I just knew I had to keep moving.

I recall falling, lying there with the sun in my eyes thinking it would blind me if I stared at it. I turned my face away and insects soon found me. I didn't care. I had no strength or will to care anymore and closed my eyes and let them feast. I just hoped it would be over soon even though I knew it would probably go on a lot longer.

After a time of the bugs crawling on me,

pausing, biting, I knew I'd go mad. I managed to shake my head from side to side when it became too much. I cursed their existence. It would stop for a while then start again. Relentless. They seemed to especially like the blood —the cuts on my hands and the one over my eye.

I struggled to get up but couldn't. I'd die just as I was. Someone would eventually find me, or what was left of me, and wonder how it came to pass a man would be like this and stories would arise and be passed from one person to another —told in saloons and quiet rooms—about the man who was found crucified to a limb.

I lay waiting for death.

Death had a peaceful voice.

I felt something working at my hands, perhaps a wolf or coyote gnawing them off. But then whatever it was did the same to the other hand and I managed finally to open my one good eye and saw the shadow of a man kneeling between me and the low sun.

"Easy, mister. Go easy."

He was dressed in black: black hat, black coat. The sunlight gleamed off his knife blade as he folded it and slipped it into his pocket.

"Who did this to you?"

I could not speak, my throat as dry as sand. I tried lifting my arms away from the limb but my shoulders seemed locked. I curled my fingers.

He raised my head and put a canteen to my mouth.

"Drink slow," he said.

It was like drinking salvation.

He trickled more water into my mouth until it had the quality and effect of oiling a machine. My tongue was swollen.

He tried to help me sit up but my scream made him ease me back down again. Then blackness came over me like a blanket.

I awoke knowing time had passed and stared into a fire lashing flames against the darkness. He sat across from it.

"Thirsty?" he said.

I nodded and again he brought me water to drink.

"How about now, you think you can sit up now?"

"I'll try." The words seemed to break in two when I said them.

He helped me sit up and I nearly fainted but managed to stay upright.

"Hungry?"

"Yes."

"Chew on this," he said and handed me some jerky.

He had a sharp bony face with close-set eyes and white hair nearly to his shoulders; he didn't seem old enough to have white hair.

"Am I dead?" I said.

"Do you think you are?"

"I don't know."

"The thing is, none of us do. We have it in our heads that we're this or that, but are we really, or is everything an illusion?"

It made no sense to me what he was saying. Maybe I was dead, or hallucinating. I closed my eyes and chewed and the jerky seemed real enough and so did the night wind and the surrounding darkness and the flames in the fire licking at the night.

I slept.

I had dreams.

I dreamt I died, that a faceless man had killed me. I awoke.

It was morning and the man in the black hat and clothes and white hair sat across from me, the fire between us.

"How are you feeling?" he said.

"Like I was just taken out of a grave."

"Born again?"

"Maybe."

His eyes were very pale, almost like colorless glass. I noticed as he reached for the coffeepot resting in the fire that he had smooth hands, the sort of hands a working man would not have, the sort of hands that a professional gunfighter or gambler would have.

"Here," he said, pouring me a cup and handing it across.

I shrugged out of my blankets and took it. It was good coffee for trail coffee.

"Who are you?" I said after taking a drink.

"Just a man in search of himself," he said, then half smiled. "And I found you, which isn't like finding me at all."

"I guess not."

"How did you get yoked?" he said. "It was an unusual sight—like a crucified man fallen from the cross."

"Maybe that's who I am, Jesus, or somebody like that. Don't it talk in the Bible about Him coming back?"

He grunted, said, "Maybe. This is strange country. I've seen lots of unusual things since I've been here, but so far you're the strangest."

"I've heard it said the land is full of spirits— that they live up on the mesas, lots of them, and that there are some who men believe can change shapes, go from men to becoming animals and vice versa."

"I've heard that too," he said. "You believe it?"

"I believe I'm not Jesus or anything close to it."

He shook his head.

"I believe that too. You want some bacon?" He took the lid off an iron skillet and the smell of fried bacon made my belly crawl. He had a Dutch oven setting on a rack over the fire and took the lid off it too and there were half a dozen small brown biscuits baked together in it and he took one out and split it apart and forked on some of the bacon and handed it to me.

We ate without saying much because I was so damn glad to have anything to eat I couldn't think to talk.

"How'd you come to be here?" I said after I ate two more of the biscuit sandwiches and swallowed down my first cup of coffee and refilled it.

"How'd you?" he said.

"Fair enough question." I told him, and he listened.

"They sound like a pretty tough bunch," he said.

"Tough enough."

I asked him if he knew where the town of Refugio was. He shook his head.

"No, I'm new to this part of the country," he said. "I came from north of here, the goldfields most recently."

"You a miner?"

"No," he said. "The farthest thing from it."

"I'm from Nebraska, myself," I said. "I sort of wish now I'd stayed there."

"I bet you do."

"I think I've got a busted rib."

He nodded knowingly.

"I think I will find what I'm looking for

here," he said, gazing at the mesas and the landscape of sage.

"Well, what you might find is trouble," I said.

"Maybe, but I think there's a reason I came here and I'm soon to find out."

"How will you know?" I said.

"I am not sure, but I believe I will know when I find it."

Sun broke over the mesas and the air was crisp and way off in the distance I could see snow-capped mountains.

"You come across a town nearby lately?" I said. "Someplace I could maybe find a horse, a pistol? Those old boys robbed me of everything I owned including some of my dignity and I aim to go and get it back, but I'll need a horse and a gun to do it."

He sat there squatting on his heels looking for all the world like a man in no hurry to be anywhere soon. He turned his head slightly.

"I came across a small village a few miles back. It was just some Mexican people mostly, a church, a cantina, some casitas. I'm not even sure of what its name was or if it even had a name."

"Which way was it and how far do you reckon?"

He shrugged. "Three or four miles, perhaps."

"Well, I might as well get started then. I'm not sure how to thank you for what you've done."

"No thanks necessary. I'm sure you would have done the same thing for me."

I'd like to think I would have but the way my life had been going, I'm not sure how much good I had in me.

I stood slowly and it hurt still and I was sore from head to toe and my shoulders ached like hell and I wouldn't have paid a nickel for me even if I had a nickel left, which I didn't. I was broke and afoot and a man in my condition couldn't get much worse off.

I started to walk in the direction he had indicated.

Then he said, "I can ride you back there," and stood himself and tossed the remains of the coffee into the fire's ashes, causing them to steam and hiss, and wiped his fry pan out with sand and put away his Dutch oven and all the rest into a large canvas sack, telling me I'd have to carry it if we were going to ride double.

He had a fine black horse—a Morgan, I'd judge—that seemed too proud to even be a horse. It stood our weight and its owner clucked his tongue and we started off at an easy walk.

We made the village in an hour and he was right about it—there wasn't much there except what he'd said was there. All the buildings were adobe and some of the casitas had strings of red chilies hanging by the front doors and brown-skinned kids played in the only street and women stood at a community well with clay pots.

"This is it," he said and stopped in front of the cantina. I slid off the horse and handed him his sack and he dismounted and lashed it behind the saddle horn.

A woman sweeping the street in front of a small casita eyed us suspiciously.

"We're probably the only white men here," he said.

"You know I didn't even get your name," I said.

"Tom Twist," he said.

"Jim Glass," I said.

"You think it matters?" he said. "The names they give us?"

"I guess it's how we know when to pay attention," I said.

He seemed to consider it.

"I guess," he said.

He was stranger than the New Mexican wind.

"I guess as long as I'm here I'll see about restocking some of my supplies," he said. Then he paused and looked at me. "You have any money?"

"No. Like I said, they took that too."

"No money, no horse," he said. "You're in quite a fix, aren't you?"

"I don't know when I've been worse off."

"Here," he said, taking a twenty dollar gold

piece from his pocket and extending it toward me.

"I'd like to be able to decline your kindness," I said. "But under the circumstances I can't."

"Take it," he said, and I did.

"Well, I wish you luck, Jim Glass—on your journey, wherever that might lead you."

"Same here, Tom." We shook hands and I watched him go up the street to a small trading post with a number of dark-skinned men sitting out front wrapped in colorful blankets.

I went inside the cantina. You want to know anything about a town, bartenders are the best people to ask.

The man behind the bar was singing to himself. That hour there weren't any drinkers. Singing and rubbing glasses with a hand towel.

"Señor," he said. He was short and fat with hair combed down over his forehead and large ears.

I was torn about buying a drink knowing every dime I had of the twenty dollar gold piece was critical to my survival.

"You speak English?" I said.

"Si. *Poquito*—a little, yes."

"Anyone in town sell horses?"

"*Cabellos*? Si. Caesar Hernandez—he have horses sometimes."

I asked directions and he told me this Hernandez had a corral at the edge of town and I thanked him and went out.

I found Hernandez squatting on the sun side of his corral, his eyes closed. He was old, his skin leathery, threads of black hair growing from his upper lip and chin. He was mumbling to himself and running a string of rosary beads through his crooked fingers.

I coughed and he opened his eyes and looked at me like an old turtle.

"I'd like to buy a horse," I said.

"I maybe have one to sell," he said.

"How much?"

He shrugged and sized me up. The wind shuffled his black hair. "You have gold or silver?"

"Gold."

That seemed to suit him and he stood up, using his hands on his knees, and shifted his serape over his shoulders and pointed to a gray inside the corral that didn't look too bad.

"That one," he said.

"How much?" I said again.

"For heem, I take forty dollars gold."

"I've got twenty," I said, showing him the double eagle.

He shook his head solemnly as though I'd just insulted his sister and was contemplating what he was going to do about it.

"Twenty, señor . . . *ayiee.* It is not enough for heem."

"What have you got for twenty?" I said.

He shook his head again. "Nothing," he said. "Maybe you could buy a big dog, eh?" He seemed to take pleasure in his own joke. I didn't think much of it.

"Let me ask you something," I said. "You know of a place called Refugio?"

"Si." He pointed a crooked finger toward a set of brown hills covered in juniper. "It's that way. Beyond those hills."

"How far?"

He shrugged. "Pretty far," he said.

Goddamn if it didn't look like he was right.

I remembered just then the reason I was standing here trying to negotiate a horse I couldn't afford: Antonia. What had happened to her? Where was she now? It was something I didn't want to think too hard about. Thinking about it just made matters worse. But I'd made her a promise and I intended to keep it.

I headed back up toward town. Somehow I had to raise more cash.

Tom Twist was just coming out of the trading post, his sack weighted down and slung over his shoulder.

"You look as lost as I feel," he said.

"Tried to buy a horse, but twenty dollars doesn't buy you much in this town."

"Wish I could help you out more, my friend, but I'm pretty well empty-pocketed myself now."

"No," I said. "You've done way more than enough."

"What were you going to do if you got yourself a horse?" he said.

"Get a gun and then probably go kill some men."

He shook his head. "Bad karma," he said.

"What?"

"It's something I learned in India. Bad actions this life make your next life more difficult."

"This is the only life I intend to live in," I said. "And I intend to get even with a few people while I can. If there's another life after this one, I'll worry about it when I get there."

His smile was close to pitying.

"Well, maybe you're not wanting a horse bad enough," he said. "And maybe the reason you don't have a horse is because it is not meant for you to seek revenge. Maybe that's not why you're here."

"You talking God, or what?" I said.

"God could be a part of it. I think it's a lot more complicated than that."

He was by any account the oddest duck I'd ever come across.

"Well, I'll tell you what," I said. "If I have to make a horse out of sticks and mud and a gun out of straw, I'm going to make sure the score gets evened."

He retied his sack to the horn of his saddle then slipped a foot into the stirrup and swung himself onboard.

"I wish you well in your journey," he said and touched heels to his mount and rode to the end of the street, where a small adobe church with whitewashed walls stood. I watched as he dismounted and, taking off his hat, went inside. It gave me pause—thinking about stealing his horse did. But I couldn't do it, after what he'd done for me.

I went into the trading post. It was cool inside with a low ceiling of plaster and ocotillo sticks. Cool and dim and I went to the counter and asked the Mexican behind it if he had any guns for sale.

"*Pistolas*, or rifles?"

"*Pistolas*," I said.

"Si."

He took out a tray with four revolvers on it. Two of them had pitted barrels and another had loose works. The last one was a Colt Thunderer—something the size a woman might carry. It had hardwood grips.

"This used to belong to Billy the Keed," he said. "I bought it from heem."

"How much you want for it?"

"Fifteen, señor."

"Five."

He shrugged and shook his head. "Twelve."

"Ten and you throw in a box of shells."

"Okay, but only half a box."

I loaded the chambers before I left and put the rest of the shells in one pocket and the last of the money in my other. I walked back down the street to the corral. The caballero looked at me like I was a lost child that had found my way home.

"You come back for the horse, eh?"

"Tell you what," I said. "I'll bet you this gun for that horse."

He looked at the gun. "It's just a gun," he said.

"It used to belong to Billy the Kid."

"So what?"

I took out the ten dollars I had left.

"How about the gun and the money?"

He shrugged. "It's not much, not enough."

I showed him my boots—new ones I'd purchased that spring in Ogallala—and the spurs to go with them. The boots had roses stitched into the shafts.

"I'll throw in my boots and spurs," I said.

"What's the bet?" He was by now nothing if not curious.

"You have a peso?"

Again he shrugged.

"You toss it in the air and if I can hit it on one try, you sell me the horse for ten dollars, and if I miss you can keep the gun, my money, my boots and spurs."

He reached in his pocket and took out a peso. The damn thing looked smaller than I'd imagined it would.

"One try," he said. "Not two."

"That's right, one shot."

He knew it was a sucker's bet and I could see in his greedy little dark eyes he was already feeling his feet inside my boots whether they fit him or not, and my ten dollars in his pocket and the pistol and all the rest.

He stepped away from the building so that we stood in sunlight.

I held the pistol in my right hand down alongside my leg.

"Go ahead," I said.

He flipped the peso high in the air and I let it land in the dirt then took aim and shot it.

"Hey," he cried. "You don't shoot it in the air."

"I never said in the air, I said I could hit it with one shot. And that's what I did."

His face bunched into brown anger.

"The hell, you're still getting ten for a horse not worth twenty," I said. I bent and took off my spurs and handed them to him. "Just to show you my heart's in the right place." It seemed to ease his pain at being suckered.

He called me a fucking gringo in Spanish as he led the horse out and handed me the halter rope. "*Gracias*," I said.

Then he called me an asshole.

159

CHAPTER FIFTEEN

A gun, a horse. What more did a man need to get by in this cruel old world? I asked myself. I probably looked pretty damn silly to the locals, riding a horse bareback with a pistol stuck down the waistband of my britches. I headed for those brown hills way off in the distance. I rode until nearly dark. The wind blew cold and I was damn near to shivering and hungry as a wolf. Ahead lay a deep purple veil of nightfall and something else. The wink of a campfire.

I rode toward it.

"Hello the camp," I called.

"Come on in, friend."

The voice sounded familiar.

It was Tom Twist there in the light, his Dutch oven steaming.

"You following me?" I said jokingly.

"Maybe I am," he said.

"Hell of a technique you have—following a man by staying ahead of him."

He offered me a plate of food.

"See you found yourself a horse after all."

"I guess I wanted it bad enough, or God wanted me to have it," I said a little sarcastically.

"Maybe so," he said with some degree of confidence.

We squatted on our heels within the heat of the fire and ate.

"You figure out where it is you're going yet?" I said after eating the stew he'd ladled onto a plate for me. It had potatoes and carrots and onions and some sort of meat chunks.

He shrugged. "Not yet, not exactly."

"Well, I'm told the way you're headed—I'm headed—will take us both right to Refugio."

"Where you were when those lawmen got hold of you," he said.

"Yes."

"And it's them you're going to kill?"

"Kill, or use pretty hard," I said. "They've got my horse, saddle, rifle, pistol, money, and some of my blood. I figure they owe me and I aim to collect."

"Might not be worth it," he said. "Results could be the same as they were last time, maybe even worse."

"They've got something else they took too," I said.

He looked at me, the light jumping on his face.

"A woman."

"Oh," he said. "Well a woman certainly does add to the drama."

So I told him the whole story, about Antonia

161

and Johnny Waco and all the rest and that what I was trying to do was something good for somebody and it had ended up costing me.

"We never do good simply for good's sake," he said. "You want some coffee?"

I nodded and he filled two cups and handed me one.

"How so?" I said.

"We mostly do good so we feel better about ourselves," he said. "Yes, we might help another person, but we don't do it for that reason alone. We do it because it makes us feel good. So it's not entirely unselfish."

"Does it matter?"

"Probably not."

"I'm guessing you were in the God business at one time or the other."

He simply smiled and said, "We're all in the God business."

Somewhere in the darkness I heard a dove coo. A moon like a china plate lifted into the night sky. Wind whispered to the fire and the fire whispered back.

"I saw you go into that church today."

"A man needs respite and replenishing sometimes," he said.

"From anything in particular?" I said.

"Most often it is from ourselves," he said. "But today was for the something else."

"You on the dodge, Tom? I mean it doesn't

162

matter one way or the other if you are. What you did for me. That's what matters."

"No," he said slowly, sipping his coffee, his brim down low over his eyes. "I'm not running from anyone except maybe myself."

"Running or searching?" I said.

"Sometimes it's the same thing."

"Sometimes it is, yes."

A star shot across the sky so quick you couldn't he sure it had.

"That a wedding band?" I said.

He looked at his hands, the ring on his finger. "Yes."

"A woman just adds to the drama," I said.

He smiled. "That it does," he said.

"You want, we can ride as far as Refugio together," I suggested.

"Maybe," he said.

I lay down by the fire, a coat and hat not much for a bed, but it was what I had. When I closed my eyes, the last thing I saw was Tom Twist squatting there holding his coffee cup between his hands, blowing on it then sipping and staring into the flames, and I wondered what all he was made of and how a man like him had drifted so far from whatever or wherever he had been.

I slept like I always did, like the dead.

"How will you do it?" he said the next morning after we'd eaten a light breakfast and cleaned the camp and mounted the horses.

"Do what?"

"Take on those lawmen by yourself?"

"I don't have all the details worked out yet," I said. "I sort of plan things as they come to me."

"Shouldn't that be important, the planning?"

"It should. I never did brag I was any sort of genius. I go along to get along, as they say. But then sometimes these things happen to you you didn't plan and you have to make it up as you go along."

"I don't think violence is the answer, Jim."

"Maybe you should tell them who committed it on me that," I said. "Wouldn't be no violence in their future if they hadn't done some in their past. I can't just let it go. And besides, there's the woman I owe."

"You can't be responsible for their behavior, only your own."

"We're square on that," I said.

We rode along.

"Turn the other cheek, is that it?" I said after thinking about it for a while.

"It takes a man of some character to turn the other cheek," he said.

"Which I don't pretend to have—character."

"Will you feel better about it later, after you've wrought violence upon them?"

"Some, I reckon. Better than I'd feel if I just let them get away with it."

We reached this side of the brown hills late

that day with clouds folding in on themselves in a low sky and the threat of rain or maybe even snow, as cold and damp as the wind was.

"We should make camp early," he said.

My whole backside was sore from riding bareback. I didn't fight him on the idea.

We made a fire and he set up his cook pot and boiled water from a clear running little stream and spilled in some beans to boil and sliced off a couple of good chunks of salted pork. We didn't talk much.

We ate and his silence was complete, as though he was preoccupied with something.

About the time I was set to lay down by the fire again he spoke.

"My wife . . ." he began. I sat there listening. "She was murdered." Wind rose and fell around us like some great beast breathing and sighing.

"It happened almost a year ago," he said, and bent and poured himself more coffee. "The men who killed her were never captured as far as I know. They're still out there somewhere . . ." His gaze looked toward a darkness as vast as an ocean.

"It's got to be hard knowing that," I said.

"It is," he said. "Annalee was a decent and kind woman. It was her kindness, I think, that cost her her life. The way it looked, what I could ascertain was, she'd let the men into the house, probably thinking to do them a kindness. There were four plates on the table, the food half eaten, muddy boot tracks under it. They probably came by and asked for a meal and she never thought anything but to feed them. She was that way—a Quaker. Peaceful woman without an ounce of hate toward anybody."

I tried imagining her, wondered if she was anything like Antonia, who I guessed was probably a good woman at one time, as all women were probably good at one time.

He reached inside his pocket and took out a silver frame and stared at it.

"That her, your wife?" I said.

He nodded and held it out and I took it and tilted it toward the light and saw the photograph of a sweet-faced woman with light hair and eyes that seemed to stare into vast nothingness; an innocent stare, it was.

"She was twenty-three," he said as I handed the picture back to him.

"Young," I said.

"She was pregnant, that was the very worst of it. I lost them both, Annalee and our child."

"I'd think you'd want to kill the men who did this," I said.

"I do," he said. "That's the problem."

"How so?"

"It goes against everything I ever believed in, everything I ever spoke out against."

"I was right then, you are in the God business."

"Was," he said. "I haven't been for a long time now. And I doubt even if I wanted to he, that I've fallen too far from the vine to be redeemed."

"Redeemed," I said. "I like that word."

He went on to tell me how he had been a preacher and had come to live among the Quakers and met his wife and fell in love with her on first sight.

"I'd been all my young life a hell-raiser till I found the Lord," he confided. "I was saved, born again, and found my own true love all within a couple of years. I was given a taste of the promised land—in her I found everything, including my true self. Then these men came along and destroyed it all and I went back to being what I was before. And now I don't know what I am. . ."

He sighed and drained what was in his cup and set it aside.

"I am lost," he said.

I felt niggardly for having been so complaining about my own circumstances now that I'd heard his.

"I'm sorry," I said. It was all I knew to say.

"So am I, Jim. So am I."

That night I had dreams of Antonia, only she had the face of the preacher's wife, those innocent eyes staring at me, and I heard the thunder of hooves and saw a rider bearing down on me. Death riding a horse. I heard a woman's scream and awoke sitting up, my pistol in my hand ready to shoot the ghosts that plagued me. But no one was there and my heart hammered inside my chest, the broken rib a painful reminder of the recent past and why I was out here now.

I lay down again and stared up at the stain of stars. All man's bloody history had been witnessed by those same stars, and all that was yet to be done would be witnessed by them as well.

The next day we rose and rode on to Refugio without talking because it didn't feel like there was anything worth saying that hadn't already been said. Nothing we needed to share about what haunted us.

We were just two men riding to an uncertain fate, pursued by bad memories, chasing uncertain things.

CHAPTER SIXTEEN

The town was as I remembered it: just a town like any other, without any sign of the violent men that it harbored.

"Well," I said to Tom, "I guess this is where I bid you farewell—in keeping with the drama of it all, of course."

His smile was slight. "I've been thinking," he said.

"About what?"

"You, those men you intend to kill or use real bad."

"Yeah, I know, pretty poor odds, and I shouldn't do to them what they did to me because it will only make me just like them, and all that."

"That's true enough. But I can't let you face them alone."

"Meaning?"

He reached back into his saddlebags and came out with a double rig and strapped it around his waist. Two-gun men were rare in the West, mostly a creation of dime novels.

"Those for real?" I said.

They had ivory handles with carvings of eagles and were nickel-plated—like something you'd see in a Wild West show.

" 'Thirty-six Navies," he said. "I bought them from a man named Utter in Colorado who said they belonged to Wild Bill, that he was trying to raise money for a headstone for Bill. They're real enough."

When he saw the uncertain look on my face he took one out—the left one—and handed it to me. I inspected it and it was the fanciest damn gun I'd ever seen anywhere. *J.B. Hickok* was engraved on the back strap.

"I bought them thinking I'd find the men who did what they did to her and kill them. But later I realized that she wouldn't have wanted that. She would rather have sacrificed her own life than that of another human being."

"But you didn't get rid of them. Why?"

He shrugged. "I guess you're lucky I didn't," is all he said.

"And you aim to do what, exactly?"

"Help you."

"You wouldn't take revenge on your wife's killers but you'd help me?"

"I wasn't able to find them, for one thing," he said. "I tried. I guess it wasn't part of my destiny to do so. I realized that if I kept trying, it would have gone against Annalee's wishes, and against whatever my fate is meant to be. It would have been futile, so I quit trying. But you're right here and you could use some help and I'm right here and I'm able to help and maybe that's what I'm supposed to do. Least, that's what it feels like I'm supposed to do."

The town looked peaceful. It was just past noon.

"We never do good just for good's sake," I said. "Isn't that what you told me the other night?"

"No, we never do," he said.

"You ever fire those things, ever shoot at a man or had one shoot at you?"

He shook his head.

"Well, I've been in a couple of gunfights," I

said. "It's something that will take your breath away if you live to tell about it."

He sat looking toward the town, down the wide main drag. Then he turned his head and looked at me.

"I think that our entire lives are laid out for us from the moment we take our first breath until the moment we take our last," he said. "If it's meant you do this thing and it's meant that I try and help you, then nothing we say or do is going to change what the outcome of this day will be. Now if you just want to sit here and keep talking about it, that's fine with me."

"I never did meet nobody like you," I said.

He simply turned his gaze toward the town again.

We rode down the center of the street and I spotted the jail to my left and I said, "That's it there" and we reined in and got down and I pulled the pistol out and held it in my right hand down alongside my leg and Tom pulled both his and followed me in. We went in fast.

The kid who'd cuffed me was reading a Bible —a small black one—and he looked up and I said, "You so much as even think about going for your gun I'm going to send you quick to heaven and you'll learn firsthand what it is like and you won't have to read about it no more. You understand?"

He nodded and looked at Tom, who had both

171

those shiny pistols aimed at him, and even I was surprised at how steady Tom held them.

"Where's your boss and the other deputy?" I said.

"Eating their lunch," he said.

"I want to know what you did with the woman."

"Sheriff Bike put her on the flyer back to Coffin Flats with a guard."

"Now that was a mistake," I said and stepped forward and cracked the butt of my Thunderer down across his hat, caving it in and knocking him half out of his chair. He let out a painful whoop and looked like he was about to cry.

"Get on back to that cell," I said.

He did as I ordered and marched back and I found a ring of keys hanging on a peg and locked him inside, and Tom came back there and handed him his Bible through the bars.

"You might want to study on it careful, what it says in there about doing unto others, son," he said.

"I ought to give you as much chance as you gave me and shoot you where you stand for leaving me to die out there," I said.

He rubbed the knot I'd put on his head and looked at his caved-in hat.

"I just do what I'm ordered," he said.

"You ought to learn better," Tom said. "Suppose you'd been ordered to fry children, or something?"

The kid deputy blinked. "Huh?"

"What do you want to do now?" Tom said to me.

"Why don't we just wait for them to come back from lunch?"

He shrugged. "It's your show," he said.

We went out into the other room where the kid had been at the desk and stood by the window looking out onto the street.

"Fry children," I said. "That's quite an image."

"Maybe it will be one that will stick with him for a while next time he's given an indecent order."

"I reckon maybe it will."

We stood around maybe thirty minutes or so.

"That's him, Joe Bike," I said, seeing the lawman and his deputy coming down the walk on the other side of the street. Bike was picking at his teeth with a thumbnail, his deputy was walking with his head down, his hands stuffed in his pockets. They stopped briefly to talk to another man, then came angling across the street to the jail. We were waiting for them, just inside the door, our pistols out.

"Come on in and close the door," I said.

Joe Bike didn't seem all that surprised to see me but his deputy did.

"How—" the deputy started to say.

"Ease your hardware out and lay it on the desk," I said.

"Or what?" Joe Bike said. "You forget I'm a goddamn sheriff?"

"Soon to be ex, or the *late,* take your pick if you don't do what I told you," I said. He looked at Tom Twist, at those pretty guns Tom was aiming at him and his deputy.

"Horace!" he called.

The one in the back said, "Yessir, I'm back here."

"I did you a favor is what I did," Joe Bike said. "I could have just as easily killed you and dropped you in a shallow grave and nobody would have known the difference."

"Yeah, you could have, but you didn't. Your mistake. Now take those guns and put them on that desk."

They eased them out and set them there.

"Where's my horse, saddle, and rifle?" I said. "And where's the money you stole off me?"

"Sold your horse and saddle and guns at auction to cover expenses," the lawman said. "And you're a liar about the money. I ain't no thief."

"Yes you are," I said and hit him square in the face—one short hard punch I'd imagined throwing for days—that knocked him back against the wall and cut his cheekbone open like I'd sliced it with a razor.

Tom stood steady with his pistols.

Joe Bike swiped at the blood running down his face, saw it on his knuckles when he looked.

"You leave a man afoot like you did me is the same thing as murdering him," I said. "I'm a man who believes in squaring things." Some of his blood dripped down onto the toe of his boot and the floorboards.

"Put that expense money and my stole money on the desk."

He snorted. "Yeah, like I've got it," he said.

"You better have it."

I thumbed back the hammer on the Colt.

He began to fumble at his pockets until he found his wallet and brought that out and took what was in there out and dropped it next to the guns. I gave a quick count. Forty dollars. I put it in my pocket.

"Now you," I said to the deputy. He took out his money and looked at it then set it down on the desk. Thirty dollars.

"My month's pay," he said.

I had no sympathy for him and took his money too.

"Now what you stole off me."

Joe Bike hesitated again and I raked him across the face with the barrel of the gun and opened another cut wider than the first one and this time he dropped to his knees, stunned.

"I can keep this up if that's what you're wondering," I said.

"You'll never make it out of this town alive," he said, wiping at his lacerated face.

"Then neither will you."

"Why don't we just kill them all right now and get it over with," Tom said. I wasn't believing what I was hearing coming from his mouth.

The two lawmen swallowed down whatever brave they still had in them.

"Okay!" Bike said. "I'll give you your money . . ."

He stood up shakily and opened the bottom left hand drawer of his desk and took out the familiar paper envelope. "It's mostly all there," he said.

"Put it on the desk and step away," I ordered.

"I still think we should just finish it here and now," Tom said. I glanced at him and saw he was looking at the lawmen like they weren't even there.

"Hold up goddamn it!" Bike protested. "You got what you came for."

I put the money into my pocket along with the rest.

"Walk on back to the cell," I said. I unlocked the door and they went in like trained puppies and I locked it on them again.

"You all know who this man is?" I said.

They looked at Tom and you could see they were trying to put his face with a name.

"John Wesley Hardin," I said. "You all are just goddamn lucky I don't let him go ahead and unload on you because there's hardly anything he likes better than killing traitorous bastards such as yourself, is there, John?"

"I've killed forty-one men," he said. "Might as well make it forty-four."

It was starting to wear on their nerves, being faced down by such a notorious bad man as John Wesley Hardin. First I was him, now Tom was him. The son of a bitch seemed to get around, even though the last I'd heard he was still in the state prison down in Texas.

"Let them live, this time, John," I said.

"I sure don't want to."

"No, it's okay. But tell you what, they make any move to come after us, we'll kill them in ways they haven't even thought of yet."

We went outside and Tom said, "Who's John Wesley Hardin?"

"A very bad man," I said.

"Oh."

"What would you have done if things had gone wrong in there? I mean you were talking tough as hell."

"Just trying to get them to cooperate with you," he said. "I don't know what I would have done if things had gone wrong. I guess we're both lucky they didn't."

"I guess."

"What now?"

"You want to see this through all the way to the end?"

"You mean getting the woman back?"

"It probably won't go near this easy," I said. "I saw what Johnny Waco and his bunch did to a city marshal and it was pretty ugly."

"You mean uglier than what you did to that sheriff?"

"By a whole lot."

"Why don't I just tag along for a time and see how it goes."

"It's your choice."

He shook his head.

"Like I said, I don't believe we have any choices, Jim." Then he seemed to consider something for a moment and said, "John Wesley Hardin. You think he'd take it as an insult that folks would mistake me for him?"

"Probably shoot you in the eyes."

He smiled then, that same thoughtful smile like someone had told him a clean joke.

"Okay," he said. "Let's go."

He was already starting up the street toward the train depot and I was already thinking I wouldn't have to ride bareback anymore like some damn bummer. But a train ride back to Coffin Flats wasn't the smart move and I stopped Tom and told him we'd have to make the trip on horseback.

He wondered why.

"Telegraph," I said. "You've heard about it, right?"

It was the first time I saw a look of impatience from him.

"Those birds we got caged will get out before we get halfway to Coffin Flats and that sheriff will wire ahead and Johnny Waco will have his boys waiting for us and probably kill us before we get both feet on the platform."

"Well then you better buy yourself a saddle and we'll resupply our food stocks."

"Let's make it quick before they all start hollering."

We found a dry goods store and I bought what we needed including a saddle and a good rifle and were out of town in under half an hour. And like it understood the situation and sided with the jailed lawmen, the weather turned meager and it began to rain.

I looked at Tom and he said, "There's a reason for everything, Jim."

Hell, what'd I know?

CHAPTER SEVENTEEN

We followed the railroad tracks. It seemed simplest. The country wasn't familiar to me and it wasn't to Tom either. We shot a jackrabbit the first night and cooked it over a fire down inside a small canyon to avoid any watchful eyes that might be roaming about. I figured by now Joe Bike and his deputies had broke jail and Johnny Waco already had gotten word I was coming.

"How's that rabbit?" I said.

Tom was chewing on it tenderly because of the heat.

"Just like a Philadelphia steak," he said.

"You've been everywhere?"

"Been around to lots of places, that is a fact."

"Asia and Philadelphia," I said. "Don't know that I ever met a man who's even been to either one of them."

"Travel seasons a man," he said.

"Your late wife, did she use to travel with you?"

"No. I did most of it way before I met her."

"You in the war?"

He nodded almost sadly.

"I was," he said. "A chaplain's assistant, in case you hadn't guessed."

"What side?"

"Union. What about you?"

"The other—the one that lost."

"It was a terrible war no matter," he said.

"It was."

"I think of the dead—especially the ones who died on the losing side of a battle—how they just got dumped into mass graves, their names unknown, their causes lost, their families never knowing what became of those lost men. Was always better if you died on the winning side . . ."

His voice trailed off, a sound fading into the distance. The rain had stopped long before and now the air was as cool as it was black and the stars were out and you could see the crescent of a moon riding a ridge of jagged mountains.

"The best friends I ever had were lost in that war," I said.

He nodded understandingly.

"We lost so much, all of us."

"At least you didn't have to kill anybody," I said. "Be grateful for that."

"Does it haunt you much, the men you killed?"

"Some. Not all the time, not every night, but now and then. Sometimes I look at a field of wildflowers and it reminds me, or sometimes, like now, sitting in the dark I'll think I hear voices out there. But not all the time, not as much as I once did."

"I prayed over a lot of those young men in their last hour," he said. "The newly wounded always cried out for their mothers, the really bad ones cried out for God. I don't know that either could or did assuage them their misery."

We ate the pieces of rabbit, cutting it up and sharing it and licking the grease off our fingers and washing it down with fresh boiled Arbuckle and there was something about it—sharing a meal like that with a man like Tom Twist, two of us different as night and day it seemed to me.

"How old were you?" I said.

"Twenty," he said. It surprised me because.he didn't look that old now except for the pure white hair. "What about you?"

"Nineteen," I said. "Hasty to get there before it was over. Went the winter of 'sixty-three, afraid I'd miss it all. Then once I got through the winter of nearly freezing to death and setting around most of it, and marching in the spring mud and got into my first foray, I couldn't wait for it to *be* over."

"I watched a lot of it with the generals," he said. "I'd go onto the field of battle afterward and do what I could to bring spiritual comfort. What they really needed were good surgeons and miracles, not my words, most of them."

"Was that when you started to doubt?" I said.

"No, I believed all the more because of what I saw. When I'd see the look that came into some of their eyes there at the very end, that look of peace just before they gave out, I knew it had to be something they saw, some sort of light, some of them said. Some spoke as though they were holding a conversation, but there wasn't anyone there but me. I remember one boy . . ." He shook his head sadly. "He was talking to somebody named James, saying, 'James, I'll be right there. Just wait there for me, James.' I looked 'round thinking somebody was there by the tent but there wasn't a soul. The boy nodded like whoever he was talking to was telling him something and he said, 'Okay, I'll do her then I'll come over there.' Then he closed his eyes and died. It happened more than once like that."

Somewhere off in the distance we heard a gunshot—too far to be concerned about, too close to ignore completely.

"I heard similar stories," I said.

"It was after that I lost my faith," he said. "After my wife."

I knew what he meant.

He took the little silver frame out again and looked at his dead wife's face for a long time then put it back in his pocket.

"I guess if you believe in those things," I said, "then you have to believe she's in a good place."

"It's what I'd like to believe and half the time I do. It's the other half the time it eats at me, my doubt does."

We lay down by the little fire knowing it would die before morning because we'd found the camp spot late and by the time we shot the rabbit and gathered some dried ocotillo wood it had grown very dark in the canyon. We didn't have enough fuel to sustain it but it didn't matter.

"Listen," I said. He lay still and I wasn't sure he hadn't already fallen off to sleep. "Any time you want to pull stakes it's all right with me. Nobody expects you to risk more than what you have already . . ."

He didn't say anything. I shut up. Speechifying in the dark wasn't my strong suit. I watched as the sliver of moon slipped beyond the ridge and the night sky looked like it was shotgunned through with stars.

I could smell the sweat and old hair oil of my hat as it lay low over my face. It seemed like I was so far away from everything and everything was far away from me. I saw a field of skulls when I closed my eyes and heard the moans of men long dead in the silence of my own thoughts. I saw the shattered woods ripped apart by cannon shot, smelled the burning flesh left after the woods caught fire, the flames ravishing those wounded who could not lift themselves to escape it. I saw a young officer speaking with a courier, his handsome face suddenly without its lower jaw, the white of his upper teeth pulsating in a bloody maw, his tongue lolling freely before he slumped off his horse into a heap.

I saw men standing in a ragged line in front of a camp whore's tent, their loneliness and lust tugging at them even though they knew the price they'd pay was two dollars and a visit to the physician's tent afterward.

I saw myself riding away on a dreary after-noon, my hunger for war sated.

Morning came without event. I went one direc-tion to gather fuel for the fire so we could eat a hot breakfast, Tom went another. The sun lit his

184

end of the canyon and I heard a shout. He came back holding his forearm.

"Snake," he said. "Big one. I should have looked where I was reaching."

He rolled up his sleeve and there on the muscled flesh two drops of blood he swiped away revealed two small prick marks.

"We need to bleed it," I said.

"Go ahead." He sat down, his face a little flushed. "Stupid me."

He handed me his Barlow knife and I opened a blade. No way to clean it but wipe it on my shirt, I took his arm and cut an X over each of the fang marks and squeezed what I could, his blood thick and reluctant.

I took off my kerchief and tied it off tight just above his elbow.

"You think you got most of it?"

I didn't know. "How big you figure it was?"

"Big," he said.

"If it gets to your heart it could be bad," I said.

"All the ways I've thought about dying, this was never one of them."

"I'll saddle our horses and we'll see if we can't find somebody to help."

He nodded and stayed sitting.

I saddled the horses and gathered our gear and we were on the move in quick time. It was wild country and we'd not yet passed a single dwelling nor saw a single trace down which a ranch might stand. We rode along at a good pace knowing that he had less than a fifty-fifty chance if we didn't find someone who could help.

An hour passed, then two. We had to rest the horses and I checked his arm and it was already swollen to twice its normal size and his fingers were fat as sausages and I said, "Does it hurt much?"

"Like you can't believe," he said, putting a brave face on it.

We rode on and still nothing but brown hills and dry riverbeds and red canyons, prickly pear and blue sky.

I saw he was having trouble staying in the saddle, swaying from side to side, his face no longer so brave; the pain etched deeply in it now, his eyes closed against it.

I rode alongside him.

"My heart's beating like a drum," he said. His face was damp with sweat.

Finally around noon we spotted a house that sat south of the tracks a half mile and made for it.

It was made of mud and stone. There were chickens in the yard and a pen of sheep. Two dogs came out barking, both of them black with white cow dogs, their bellies low to the ground. A man was grinding an ax blade on a stone wheel and looked up when the dogs began barking. He stopped turning the wheel and stood up holding the ax. A woman who was bent at the waist in a field of pumpkins also stood and looked in our direction.

The man reached for a rifle he had leaning against the grinding wheel.

I raised an open hand as we rode up, holding the reins of Tom's and my horse in the other. Tom was barely hanging on, lying low over his saddle horn.

"My friend's been bitten by a big rattler," I called soon as I stopped our horses. "He needs help."

The man looked at us suspiciously then set his ax down but held onto his rifle.

"Maize," he called, and the woman stepped out of the pumpkins and walked to where we were.

I dismounted and helped Tom out of the saddle. The man looked at his arm, said, "Jesus!" Then, "Bring him inside."

The woman held the door for us and the man pointed toward a cot in the corner of the front room. Besides the cot, there was a kitchen stove with three burner plates, a table, two chairs, cupboards, and a dry sink.

Tom groaned when I eased him down.

"When'd he get bit?" the man said, looking closer at Tom's arm.

"This morning."

The man stood and went to the cupboard and got a long thin-bladed knife and a bottle of liquor and came and pulled a chair up close to the bed.

"I'm going to cut your arm, mister" he said to Tom. Then to me, "You two help hold him."

The woman moved to the head of the bed and placed her hands on Tom's shoulders and bore down and I held his other arm as the man drew two long slits with his knife down the length of Tom's forearm. The blood rushed out and the man pulled the cork on the bottle with his teeth and spilled the whiskey into the cuts. Tom jerked like he'd been shot.

"Get me some bandages, Maize," the man said. She left and then returned with several strips of muslin.

The man reached in his shirt pocket and took out a twist of tobacco and bit off a good chunk and chewed and took a sip of the liquor and kept chewing with the liquor in his mouth till he had a good wad then compressed it to the bite marks and wrapped a strip of muslin to hold it into place, his fingers bloody from the work.

Then he said to Tom, "Drink some of this," and held the bottle to his mouth and Tom swallowed some of it down.

"That's about all I know how to do for him," the man said. "Hoping the tobaccy will draw the poison out." Tom's eyes fluttered. "Maize, wench up some cold water and soak cloths and put them on his arm clear up to the shoulder. The cold will slow down his blood." The woman left the house and came back in several minutes with a bucket of water and set about bathing Tom's arm and shoulder.

The man motioned me outside.

"I din't want to say it in there where he could hear me, but your friend's going to die, mister."

"No he's not," I said.

He shrugged.

"Bad break," he said. "Hard country. You want a taste of this?" He handed me the bottle. I took a pull and handed it back.

"How far from here to Coffin Flats?" I said.

He shrugged. "Another two days you keep at it steady. That where you're from?"

"It's where I'm going."

He wore a thin coat. Dark-skinned. Could have had some Mexican or Indian in him; the woman too.

"I thought when I first saw you two coming you were Clancy's men."

"Who's Clancy?"

"A one-eyed son of a bitch," he said.

The sheep in the pen bleated plaintively, the dogs paced restlessly.

"You want you can go on alone," he said. "Maize and me will see to your friend, bury him when he's passed."

"He's not going to need burying," I said.

He took another pull off the bottle and offered it back to me but I declined and he punched the cork back into the neck with the heel of his hand

and set it next to him where he squatted on his heels looking at his sheep.

"I need to get them sheep up to Clancy's Crossing and load them on the train and send them to market," he said.

"The same one-eyed son of a bitch, Clancy?" I said.

"Yeah, he's got the market on things round here. All but me and Maize. Wants to buy me out. I won't sell. Hell, where would I go? Where would she?"

"Your wife and you?"

He shook his head.

"Sister," he said. "This place is all we got. My old man fought the Apaches for it and his old man fought them too and was killed by them. Thank God they're all over in San Carlos and we don't have to fight them no more."

The woman came out of the house and the man stood and I stood with him. It was the first I really paid any real attention to her. She was of an age most would consider spinster—plain but not bad looking.

"He's asleep," she said, shaking her head. "I can't tell if he's any better or not."

"I got to get them sheep to Clancy's Crossing," the man said again.

"I can help you get them there," I said.

"No, you stay on with your friend. I can get them there just fine."

"It's no problem," I said.

"No, I got the dogs."

He looked at the woman.

In a short while we watched him head off with his band of sheep, his two dogs working to keep them bunched and moving. He carried the rifle over his shoulder.

"You hungry?" she said.

"I could eat."

She fixed a pot of mutton stew with wild onions in it and we sat across from each other, her eyes lowered most of the time, which gave me a chance to observe her closer. She had a broad face with wide-set eyes. Her dark hair was parted in the middle and roped into braids that hung down to her breasts. Her nose was straight and her lips looked like they'd been finely carved, just right to fit the rest of her face. She had thick hands. She ate with a delicacy as if she were eating in the finest restaurant in a city. I'd seen women with large hats eating that same delicate way. When I finished she asked if I wanted another helping.

"Thanks but no," I said.

"Big man like you should eat more," she said in an almost motherly way.

I didn't know what to say.

She cleaned up the dirty dishes and gathered everything on a sideboard at the sink. "I can dry those plates if you like," I said when she came back from outside with a pail of water she filled a pan with.

"It's not necessary," she said.

"Are you and your brother always so independent you won't accept no kind of help?"

She smiled. "Okay," she said. "The towel is right over there."

We stood washing and drying and I liked how that felt. She stood about as tall as my shoulder.

I checked on Tom when we finished the dishes and he was still asleep, but moaning some, and I couldn't be sure but his arm didn't look any worse than it did before and maybe some better. She made us coffee and we went outside to drink it and the sun glazed brightly beyond the distant mountains that looked so faded as to be clouds on the horizon.

"You like living way out here?" I said.

"No, not really," she said. "But here is where we are."

I tried to guess why a woman would live so far out from anybody, not have herself a man, houseful of kids running around.

"Always just been you and your brother?" I said.

"How do you mean?"

"Have you ever been married?"

"No," she said, shaking her head. "It would have had to have been some lonesome cowpoke, or some no account drummer—way out here;

that's about all you ever see this far from town. Why marry something you know you're not going to stick to?"

"You mind I ask about the trouble between your brother and Clancy?"

She shrugged.

"It's pretty simple," she said. "He wants to buy Spence and me out, resents we haven't sold to him. Our place sets right in the middle of the rest of his holdings. He has to run his cattle around the long way. And besides, he hates sheep and those who keep them."

"Why not sell, since you don't care for it all that much?"

"I don't, but Spence does."

"You never got the urge to strike out on your own?"

"Just about every day. But I couldn't leave Spence here to fend for himself."

The wind played with the dust by the empty pen.

"What about you?" she said. "You got a woman kept off somewhere?"

"No. If I had, I'd be with her."

She sipped her coffee, looking at me over the rim of her cup, something in her eyes telling me something, conveying something unspoken but something a man should know when he sees it in a woman's eyes.

"He won't be back till tomorrow afternoon,"

she said. "He'll get his sheep to the loading station then get a good drunk on, probably buy himself a woman and stay the night. Buy supplies in the morning and come home."

She looked off toward the direction he had gone with the sheep and dogs.

"What about you, you ever go into town for fun?"

"No kind of fun in Clancy's Corners for a girl like me to have," she said. "Unless it's she enjoys wrassling with dirty shirt cowpokes who'd treat her like the morning flyer—all wanting to stand in line and get on board. I never had any urges to be the morning flyer."

"Anything that you do for fun?"

"You asking me to show you?"

"Maybe I am."

She turned and looked at the door of the house.

"I'm not loose," she said. "But I *am* damn lonely."

"I know the feeling," I said. "Seems a little foolish we both are when we wouldn't have to be."

"Let me think on it some."

"Sure," I said.

I spent the rest of the afternoon taking care of the horses, lounging about, uncertain as to where things were headed, concerned about how Tom was making it, whether or not he'd live or I'd end up leaving him in this place. It felt like I

194

knew him a lot longer than I had. I didn't want to think about his dying before I got to know him better.

She and I ate a supper of the same stew. She did not speak but simply looked at me, judging, weighing the possibilities in her mind. I was doing the same and we both knew it every time we looked at each other. We washed and dried the dishes after she got Tom to eat a little bit.

"There's a water hole not far from here," she said. The sun was low over the mountains so all you could see was its light thrown up against the evening sky.

"You ever bathe naked with a woman?" she said.

"A time or two," I said.

"I've had in my mind some time now how I'd like to bathe naked with a man in the moonlight," she said.

We took some towels and a bar of soap and stepped out into the evening air, which was cool now but not intolerable. The sky with the sunlight drained out of it had turned a dark blue metal. I followed her down to the waterhole beyond sight of the house. It was a large flat pan of red rock where a stream ran in from higher up and drained away from the lower end, leaving a natural pool in the middle the water had worn into a bathtub over a thousand years or more. A full moon had risen and seemed so close we could just reach out and rub our hands over its surface. I watched her undress, dropping her clothes casually until she stood fully naked. Then she unbraided her hair and shook it free and half turning to me said, "You just going to stand there and watch?" Then she walked into the water up to her waist.

I stripped out of my duds and walked in to where she stood and I was surprised that it felt warmer than the air. She said it was from the sun heating it all day.

"You sure are white," she said, laughing as she led me into the deepest part of the pool.

I felt like being led.

"You've done this before."

"All the time," she said. "Only alone."

We naturally came together, her head inclined, and I kissed her wet mouth. She urged her body even closer to mine when I did, floated up against me, and everything after that just took its natural course. The weight of her was hardly anything at all, buoyed by the water as I held her, suspended, floating in my arms it seemed. She laughed and kissed my face and lips and neck. I did my best to please her.

"Like that," she whispered. "Just like that . . ."

Later we used the soap to wash each other and it felt like we were children playing and the moon reflected itself in the pool all around us. Then we rinsed and climbed out onto the still warm rock and dried ourselves with the towels and dressed then walked back to the house.

Tom was sitting up at the table, his swollen arm resting atop it, a cup of coffee near his good hand.

"I wondered where you had gone," he said, then looked at Maize, her hair still wet, and said, "Oh . . ."

"How are you feeling?" I said.

"Like I want you to cut my arm off."

"Least you're not dead," I said. "I'd think you would be by now if you were going to be."

"There's worse things than death," he said. "I know that now."

"You think you'll be up to riding tomorrow?"

He shook his head. "I don't know. I'm still feeling dizzy and sick."

Then he asked if I could help him lay down again. I did. And the house had gone quiet. And when Maize snuffed the lamp there by her bed, we lay in the darkness of moonlight.

"I'd like to try that again," she said. "What we did in the water. Only slower this time."

"I was hoping you'd say that," I said.

We could hear the silence of time shifting, and later I could hear her heart beating as steady as a good watch and it brought me peace.

CHAPTER EIGHTEEN

From the diary of Maize Walker . . .

July 17, 1881.
Dirt, desert, wind, sky. Days all the same, except sometimes it rains in the summer months when the heat is at its zenith. Spence and me sometimes sit out in it just for relief as we did today. Spence believed it was as hot as it's ever been.

April 3, 1882.
I watched a spider build its web. A construction so fine it seems unimaginable.

May 11, 1882.
Spence gone to town with sheep, am here alone. Sing all day so I can hear the sound of a human voice. In town he will take part of the sheep money and buy himself liquor, a woman. He never talks about it except sometimes in his sleep. Last time he cried out the name "Ismeralda" and I could hear him banging around in his room.

October 22, 1882.

Bleeding nine days now, unusual. No doctor near to consult. One at Consideration River—90 miles. No pain, but feeling weak.

November 1, 1882.

Have harvested the pumpkins. More than we need. Spence says he'll take a load to Clancy's Corners and try and sell them. The biggest took the two of us to lift in the cart. Spence wanted to know what I was feeding them. Sometimes he makes me laugh.

She likes best writing at first light as Spence goes about his business, as the two dogs follow after him, as the world is still sleeping. On a shelf, the image of a man in a silver frame with a long tangled beard, his eyes staring into the lens like a man about to be executed. Hayes Walker, grandfather, who died grimly (found with several arrows in his body) seems to keep a watchful eye on her. In death, his face was more relaxed than in the photographer's studio in Santa Fe.

December 29, 1882.

Would you believe it snowed? Went out in it, let the flakes fall upon my face, like cold kisses, so lightly they tickled.

December 31, 1882.
*Last day of the year and have a cold & fever.
Up all night sick. Spence agrees to go get
doctor in Consideration River if I need him.
Decide to wait another day.*

January 7, 1883.
*Saw a badger today near swimming rock
drinking. Its eyes fierce. I told Spence & he
went in search of it and tonight we'll have
badger stew instead of mutton. I'm not so
sure it will taste as good, but a change
nonetheless.*

Occasionally a rider or drummer would come
by—men on their way to somewhere else—and
they would give her knowing looks as if to say:
"I know lonely when I see it in a woman and
I'm available if you're in need of a man."
Once it was a young rider whom she feared
was on the dodge from trouble, his black shirt
spanked with dust.

April 19, 1883.
*A young man who calls himself Tate
Harrison arrived at noon today, his horse
all lathered. A blue-eyed boy of no small
beauty with dark ringlets of hair cascading
from under his hat to his shoulders.
Hospitality assured he'd be invited to stay*

for dinner. I was tempted to invite him to my bed as I had done on one or two other occasions—the patient-medicine drummer the summer before, and Henry Stob, that time he came with a load of Hay and Spence was gone hunting. But something warned me about young Mr. Tate—that he was dangerous in the extreme. Not that he would do harm to me anywhere except the possible ruination of my heart. He was quiet and had the sweet soft mouth any girl would be jealous of. Now past midnight and I am still awake thinking about him, my skin crawling with the memory of his eyes looking at me across the table at supper. He rode away right after.

August 22, 1883.
Henry Stob asked if I wanted to marry him. Wife dead not three months and already he is looking for a new one. Claims he can't stand living alone and can't cook nor clean house very good. Of course I told him no. He seemed so forlorn, wanted me to take him to my bed again. No, again. He wanted to know why not when I had once already. How does a woman explain to a man that what she does she doesn't always do for love alone? Told him instead I hoped for a younger man who could give me children.

He did not seem to understand, swore a vow his seed was still good. Went away dour.

When the heat became too intense to work for long periods, she would go to the swimming rock and there remove her clothes and slip into the pool of water, letting it slide over her skin like cool silk. She would soak until her bones grew cool and think of a life unlived. She would like to have children before she grew too old. But where to find a proper man? And closed her eyes in wistfulness.

Some days she did not write in her diary.

Some nights she did not dream.

Some hours she did not think of the children she did not have.

September 30, 1885.
Two riders rode up to the house today, one of them with a hurt arm—bitten by a snake. Arm and hand swollen something terrible. Spence did what he could by cutting and applying tobacco poultice but feels certain the fellow will not live.

The other one is quite handsome and about the right age. Am considering asking him to go for a swim with me if opportunity presents itself. He seems likable.

CHAPTER NINETEEN

Day broke. The woman slept beside me. Our lust less now that it had been spent, ardor cold as ashes. I rose from the bed without waking her and went in to check on Tom. He lay on his side with his face to the wall. It hit me then that he might be dead. But when I touched him he rolled over.

"How you feeling?" I said.

He looked at me standing with a blanket wrapped around me.

"How you?" he said.

"Fair to middling."

"I guess I'm about the same. Arm feels some better, not as tight." I couldn't see much difference when I looked.

He said, "Help me sit up." He held his ravished arm tenderly as I helped him.

"Jesus," he said. "I'm so dizzy I can't see straight."

"Just take it easy."

"Don't worry, I'm not planning on wrestling you."

"You want coffee?"

He nodded.

I shuffled over and found the tin of Arbuckle

and then went out and pumped a pot of water and shuffled back in again. The morning was cool and bright and I didn't see any sign of Spence having returned.

I started a fire in the stove and set the coffee to boiling.

"You think maybe you should put some clothes on before her husband gets home?" Tom said. He looked pale, like someone had scrubbed all the color out of him.

"They're brother and sister," I said.

"Well, that's a positive note," he said. "Still, do you think he might be a little upset, the two of you having just met?"

"Point taken," I said, and shuffled back into her room and began to dress as quietly as I could.

My back was to the bed when she said, "You leaving, Jim?"

I was pulling on a boot, trying to balance myself.

"Just thought I'd get dressed. Get some coffee going and check on Tom."

She sat up, her long hair covering the dark buttons of her bare breasts, and I noticed again how well formed she really was—not one of those thin, fine-boned women like Antonia or Fannie, but of sturdier stock, like a woman who was built for hard and practical work all her life. I hadn't been looking for that in her the night before, her beauty was of its own kind and not of the classical variety.

"Nothing to hold you," she said, "if you *did* want to leave. Certainly not me." It felt awkward talking to a naked woman and me half dressed.

"Never thought of you as the sort of woman to try and hold a man if he didn't want to stay," I said.

"Something struck me as odd, Jim."

"What's that?"

"You never called me by my name—not once."

"Maize," I said.

"That's better," she said with a smile. "It would be nice if you kissed me good morning. Not required, but nice."

"I'm sorry, Maize. I guess I'm acting like a damn dote." I bent and kissed her.

"Thank you," she said, and rose from the bed without trying to hide anything and began to dress and I had a hard time taking my eyes off her because she was so natural about herself and it wasn't every day you saw that in a woman either.

We went out together and Tom was still sitting there holding his arm and looking miserable.

"Which way is your privy?" he said.

"Out back and beyond the hill," she said.

"You need help getting to it?" I said.

"Let me give it a go on my own. I'm not back in an hour, bring a shovel and bury me."

He rose unsteady and walked out barefoot.

"I like him," she said.

"I do too."

"You brothers?"

"No. Just friends."

"I didn't think you were kin. You don't look anything alike. He looks like butter and you look like hard rock."

"If that's meant to be a compliment, thank you," I said. She smiled at that.

We ate breakfast of warm biscuits, honey, slabs of fried ham, hash, hot coffee. Jim didn't eat much but he ate some. Said he was still feeling tenuous—*tenuous!*—from the poison.

"I knew a woman once who killed three of her husbands by poisoning them," he said. "Now I know what they must have felt like."

Maize looked amused.

"You think you're up to riding today?" I said.

He shook his head. "I think it would be better if I waited another day." Then he turned and looked at Maize and said, "If it wouldn't be too much trouble for you, miss?"

She looked at me with an unsettled smile.

"No, no trouble at all."

Tom said he'd like to sit out in the sun, that he felt cold in his blood. We took a chair out and placed it where the sun was best and he sat in it and closed his eyes and lifted his face and said, "That feels a lot better."

Maize went inside and I stayed with Tom.

"I'm sorry I'm dragging you down," he said. "I know you want to get to Coffin Flats and save that woman."

"Another day isn't going to matter," I said.

"You don't have to wait for me," he said.

"I know I don't."

He closed his eyes again. Parts of his arm were black and red like overripe fruit, like a plum split open. He hadn't died, but he could still lose his arm. I didn't know what was worse for a man, to die or lose a part of himself. I hoped I'd never have to face that choice.

I thought I'd give it another day or two and then if he still wasn't up to going with me I'd go on alone. I didn't want to abandon him after he'd thrown his lot in with me, but I didn't want to abandon Antonia either. I couldn't even imagine what she might be going through at the hands of Johnny Waco, especially after she'd run off from him a second time. I hoped he wouldn't be son of a bitch enough to break her hands like he had Chalk Bronson's.

There were plenty of worse things I imagined a man like him could think to do to punish her.

I passed the morning currying the horses and splitting large pieces of cottonwood Maize said her brother had sawn and dragged up to the house and left there to cure. Working the ax felt good to my muscles but reminded me too of the broken rib that hadn't healed all the way and still pinched when I didn't swing just right.

The air was pleasant and a man could work up a hell of an appetite in no time at all. Maize worked in her pumpkin patch and I walked out and did some hoeing with her.

"Did you know that Geronimo raised pumpkins?" she said.

"Interesting."

"The Apaches owned all this at one time, Lipans, Chiracahuas."

"Your brother told me all about his old man and Grandpa fighting them for it."

"They killed Grandpa over it. Father found his body in a canyon shot so full of arrows he looked like a porcupine. That's his photograph inside the house."

She wiped her face with the hem of her apron.

"The funny thing is, we got some Indian in us too, Spence and me, and all us Walkers, going way back. Cherokee, I think."

"I was wondering," I said.

She leaned on her hoe handle.

"Look at all of it," she said. "All this land. You'd think there's enough for everybody to live on, but it doesn't seem there ever is. Seems like folks are always fighting over it, wanting to fence off their portion and keep others off. Even Spence, when it comes down to it. He doesn't want Clancy to cross it with his cattle and Clancy doesn't want us on it with our sheep. And nobody wanted the Indians on it . . ."

I glanced to where Tom was sitting, his head down now, no doubt dozing, his arm lying in his lap like a useless thing.

"I guess it's just something in folks," I said. "To fight over what they believe is theirs— whether it's land or a woman or whatever."

"You ever fight over a woman?" she said.

"No."

"Land?"

"Never owned any."

"I thought not. You don't seem the type to fight over a woman, but let a woman fight over you."

I smiled at that.

"I don't know of any women who's ever fought over me, or if they have I sure never knew about it."

She laughed and I did too.

"And you *sure* don't look the kind who would own something he'd plant his feet in."

"Just never came across anything I thought was worth owning," I said.

We worked till noon and took a break for lunch and then she said, "Spence should have been back by now." There wasn't any real alarm in her voice, but there was a dark thread running through it.

"Maybe he got a bigger drunk on than usual," I said.

"Maybe."

We ate dinner outdoors, our plates resting on our laps, the sun angled straight overhead. Afterward Tom said he was tired and would like to lie down and he went inside the house.

"Want to take a walk with me, Jim?"

We walked down to the waterhole. In the sunlight the water looked green around the edges, darker in the center where it was deepest. We sat on the warm rock and kissed and leaned back and held each other.

"I could get used to this," she said.

I didn't say anything.

"My time's running out, Jim."

"For what?"

"Children."

Again I didn't say anything.

She sat staring into the water and I didn't know what to make about her comment but I had an idea where she might be headed.

"That what you want, children?"

"It's been something on my mind. But without a proper man . . ."

"I wouldn't be him, Maize."

"Oh, of course you wouldn't, Jim."

"I don't even know who I am," I said. "Don't know how I'd be able to let someone else know me enough to trust me with such responsibility. Kids need someone they can count on. I've never worked steady in my life or stayed too long in one place. It isn't something I plan, just something that has worked out that way."

She smiled.

"It was just a thought that come to me is all," she said. "I didn't mean to imply nothing by it. I'm sorry."

"No need to apologize."

A soft wind wrinkled the water. The few clouds that floated overhead were mirrored in the green surface. "You want to go for a swim?" I said.

"No, I guess not."

Whatever had been there between us, that feeling two people have when they're new to each other, when there is a mutual hunger, wasn't there any longer. Whatever it was had passed and we both knew it wouldn't come back again, that no words or actions could make it like it was for that brief time.

"Want to just sit here then?" I said.

She nodded.

You could see dusk coming half an hour before it arrived, like purple dust. Maize kept going outside the house and looking toward the north.

"He should have been home before now," she said the last time she came in again, this time with worry in her voice. "He's never been gone this long." Darkness had dropped down all around us.

"Maybe because he knows there are men here he might have seen it as a chance to take a little extra time away," I suggested.

"No," she said. "It's not Spence's way. He's a homebody. Whatever fun he wanted to have, he's had it by now. Something's wrong."

"You want me to go and try and find him?"

She looked at me with eyes that begged the question but she remained silent.

"I'll go," I said.

"I don't want to put you out."

"You've done plenty enough for us."

Tom was sitting there at the table, some of the color back into his face, his swollen arm resting next to his cup, his fingers still fat.

"It's no use going tonight," she said. "If something's happened to him along the way you won't find him in the dark. If he's not home by morning . . ."

"I can leave now."

"No. Maybe he'll come tonight. If not you can go in the morning. If something's happened and he's fallen along the way, you'll be able to spot him."

"You sure you don't want me to go right now?"

She nodded.

We all went to bed early, only this time I slept on the floor by the stove and Maize didn't say anything about it when I suggested it.

But sometime during the night she came and lay next to me and took my arm and put it around her and I pretended that I didn't hear her crying softly.

CHAPTER TWENTY

I was already up and saddling my horse when Maize came out of the house carrying a cup of coffee she handed to me. Bunches of gray clouds had gathered off to the north and it looked like they had rain in them, and a cold wind blew loose sand and rolled tumbleweeds across the open places.

I took the coffee from her and sipped it and our eyes met and held for a moment.

"Don't worry," I said. "I'll find him and bring him home."

"I know you will."

She put her hands over mine as I held the cup, an embrace of friendship more than love, it seemed to me. Comforting.

"About yesterday and what happened the night before . . ."

"It was what it was," I said. "I don't regret it and I hope you don't either."

"No," she said. "I don't regret it either, Jim."

I asked her for directions to Clancy's Corners —the direction Spence would have gone, and she gave them to me.

"It's just a place with a whorehouse, a saloon, small trading post, and a loading pen for the train when it stops," she said. "If he's there you'll be able to find him."

I nodded and drank the rest of the coffee and tightened the cinch and slid my rifle into the scabbard then forked the saddle.

"Tom's better," I said. "He was awake when I checked on him."

"I'll see to him," she said. "And thank you."

"No thanks necessary, Maize. If we aren't anything else, we are at least friends. You and Spence."

She touched my knee and I handed her back the cup then rode off toward the north.

It was about five miles, she said, from their place to Clancy's Corners. I looked for his body along the way, one of his dogs perhaps, anything that might indicate he never made it there, or made it back. I didn't see anything until I saw a few buildings below as I topped a slight rise of loose rock and sand. There were the railroad tracks, a water tower, a large wood pen, and two buildings that looked like hastily thrown together shacks. The place had the look of impermanence, like in a few years it wouldn't be there anymore; that it would all be blown away and forgotten and nobody would remember it ever having been there.

I rode down cautious, not knowing what to expect.

There were several saddle horses tied up out front of one of the buildings. No sign or nothing to indicate what it was. Just some scoured gray boards nailed together under a rusted tin roof. The stock pens were empty, the tracks quiet, their worn steel rails dull in the cloudy light.

I tied off and went in.

Several men, the number matching the number of horses out front, stood at a rough plank board propped on two wood barrels on one side of the room. The opposite side looked like a dry goods —the trading post, I assumed, Maize had spoken of. A man in a plug hat stood behind the plank bar pouring liquor from a bottle into one of the glasses in front of the men. They all looked up when I came in. None of them looked friendly.

I said, "I'm here looking for Spence Walker."

Their eyes fell on me like I'd come to collect taxes.

Nobody said anything. So I repeated myself, something I hated to do.

The man behind the bar in the plug hat had sideburns like tangled wire that came down to his chin. He wore a black eye patch over his right eye.

"Spence Walker, you say?"

215

I walked up to the bar.

"I'm a friend of his," I said. "You must be Clancy."

He looked at me close with the only eye he had like he was trying to see through water, his eyebrows bunched. He had an odor like something old and sour with a hint of cheap perfume mixed in. His striped shirt was soiled with dark stains all down the front like spilled coffee or tobacco juice.

"That's right," he said. "I'm Clancy and I own everything your eye falls on 'round here and Spence Walker is no friend of mine."

You could feel men tighten their shoulders, shift in their boots. It was like some sort of threat but it wasn't, quite.

"So I heard," I said. "His sister's worried about him. Sent me to look for him. That's what I'm doing, looking for him."

One side of his mouth curled into a cur-dog smile showing a broken eye tooth, and he poured whiskey in a glass and pushed it forward with the tips of stubbed fingers missing the first joints.

"Have a drink, stranger. On the house this one, but you buy the next."

"I don't drink before breakfast," I said. I could see he wasn't used to being turned down. "But I'll make an exception this time." I tossed the drink back and it was something like you might imagine if you were to drink coal oil.

"Better give me a beer to chase that nasty sumbitch down," I said.

He seemed to enjoy my discomfort and said to one of the men at the bar, "Farge, piss in that empty glass so this man can have himself a warm beer." Then looked at me and added: "Farge here is our beer manufacturer."

Farge was obviously the oaf who took a big glass mug off the bar top and undid himself and took a hearty piss into it then handed to me. I took it and held it aloft, as though to judge its quantity and quality, then swung it in a swift downward arc, smashing it against the side of the oaf's head so hard it rained piss and broken glass all over that dull smiling face. At the same time I was swinging the mug I pulled the pistol from my belt before the oaf fully hit the floor and jabbed the muzzle against Clancy's eye patch before he could finish hooting.

"Now you stupid bastard, tell me where Spence Walker is or there's going to be a new owner of everything my eye falls upon."

The others in the place shuffled back like I just announced I had the plague.

Clancy jerked his head back so hard his hat fell off but I grabbed him by the front of his shirt so he couldn't go anywhere and cocked the hammer back. The oaf lay out cold on the floor, no doubt dreaming of some past glory he never had, his pecker shrunk back in his trousers like the neck of a turtle.

"He come yesterday and loaded them damn stinking sheep on the train," Clancy said, his eye bulging. "Kellogg paid him then he went and bought him a gal at the Cajun's is all I know."

"Where's the Cajun's?"

"Cross the way there by the water tower."

"I'm leaving now," I said. "Don't try and fool with me or I'll ruin your day. And if I find out different about Spence, that you're lying to me, I'll be back."

I backed out of the place knowing they probably would not *fool* with me. You judge a man by his actions not his talk, and I'd shown them I wasn't about a lot of talk.

The only other building that looked habitable was a small adobe standing in the shadow of the water tower. I was still trying to work that terrible taste out of my mouth from the oily liquor.

I wrapped on a heavy wood door and waited until it opened and a skinny woman who looked like she'd just gotten out of bed stood there in a dingy nightgown.

"We don't do no business before noon," she said. "Come back then."

She started to close the door but I wouldn't let her.

"I'm looking for Spence Walker," I said.

"And I'm looking for a rich husband, honey, and if you find one let me know."

"If Spence is inside, send him out, I want to talk to him."

I heard a masculine voice with a thick accent ask, "Who dat at dey door?"

She turned her head and said, "Some damn cowboy is here looking for Spence."

"Tell him he can go fuck himself."

"He said to go fuck yourself, mister." She seemed to find her relay amusing until I shoved her aside and went in. A consumptive looking man sitting in a chair with a blanket around his shoulders smoking a pipe seemed lost in a cloud of blue smoke. I didn't give him a chance to set the pipe aside but instead slapped it from his skeletal hands.

"I come for Spence and I'm not leaving here without him," I said.

The woman started cursing me, asking what right I had to bust in and lay down threats, and I told her to shut the hell up, and she did when she saw I was serious.

The man looked at me dully as though I were some apparition he couldn't quite believe in, possibly a dead relative or the like.

"Spence?" he said. "Who dey fuck is Spence?"

"Oh, honey, you know Spence," the woman said. "That stinking sheepherder comes around here to plink Carmella."

"Sheep," he cackled. "Carmella? Where dey sheep?" And he looked 'round like a kid at Christmas trying to see where the presents were hid.

The place smelled of sex and worse.

"Come and gone, Spence is," the woman said. "Was here yesterday, bought himself two pokes off Carmella and left."

It didn't sound right, what she was telling me, what everyone in the Crossing had told me so far.

I saw a door and went and threw it open and there was a naked brown woman sleeping face-down on a narrow cot.

"Carmella," the other woman said. "You satisfied? He ain't here."

I went outside again. The wind was blowing hard, throwing sand up against the buildings, rattling the pen rails. The spout on the water tank swung back and forth. The clouds had lowered themselves threateningly. I looked about. Nothing but a spot in the road. Then I saw something small limping way off on the far side of the tracks. A black and white dog. I went to get my horse. Clancy and the others were standing out front of the storefront, some holding drinks, curious to see what I'd do, as though they had all bought tickets to some theater spectacle.

I mounted without acknowledging their presence and rode across the railroad tracks out a couple hundred yards to where I'd seen the limping dog.

I found the dog licking the hand and face of Spence Walker, who looked like someone had tossed him from a moving train. His face and hands were bloody, his clothes torn, one of his dogs lay dead a few feet away. I washed the shepherd's face with canteen water and he opened his eyes and looked at me.

"Spence, it's me, Jim Glass."

"Oh," he said.

I checked to see if he'd been shot anywhere. He hadn't.

"What happened to you?" I said.

He shook his head. "I ain't sure."

"Can you stand?"

"No, Jim, I think something's wrong with my foot."

I looked down and saw his one foot was turned wrong.

"I'll be back," I said, and rested his head down gently again and forked the saddle and rode back toward the Crossing, pulling the rifle from the scabbard as I went.

I don't know what made me say it other than I was pissed off they'd do this to a man then just let him lay there. I knew what it was like to be such a man. When I reined in short of the storefront I said, "I am the Redeemer, the swift sword, the slayer of evil! And you sons a bitches better get that man a horse and whatever money you stole from him and go and bring him here to me, or I'll start killing you where you stand!"

It was like a sudden hard wind knocked them all back on their heels as my horse danced around, my rifle held in my hand. And when they did not move fast enough to suit me, I shot out the only plate-glass window in that snake-head whiskey joint and it crashed raining glass.

"Do it, boys!" Clancy himself said. "Jeez Christ, mister, what the fuck is wrong with you?"

I aimed the rifle at him and said, "You're about to find out if you don't do what I tell you."

Several of them took a wagon out and came back with Spence in the back with his dog. Spence looked confused. One of the men untied a saddle horse standing out front and handed me up the reins and those in the wagon lifted Spence onto the horse's back then lifted him up his lame dog and I looked at Clancy and said, "Where the hell's his money for the sheep he sold?"

"He spent it on whores. Go ask the Cajun."

"I will burn this trash heap to the ground and scatter you like the wind."

Clancy reached in his jacket pocket and came out with an uncertain amount of money and handed it to Spence, who took it without question and pocketed it. He'd lost his hat somewhere. It wasn't important. He could buy another one.

"I'll be staying out there awhile, my friend and I, in case you're thinking to seek your own redemption," I said to Clancy. "My friend's name is John Wesley Hardin and mine is Jim Glass and I've murdered almost as many men as he has. We got this running bet going—who can kill more men. So far he's ahead, but I aim to catch up fast. Keep your men at home or you'll be burying them like winter potatoes." It was about the longest speech I ever gave anyone. They took it like kids to medicine.

I spanked the rump of Spence's horse with the barrel of my rifle and waited till he was well started south again, then I followed and didn't bother to look back. I wanted them to think I was invincible, and by God I think they must have thought that because no one tried to follow us.

Tom was sitting in the yard when we rode up, and Maize was hanging fresh washed clothes on a line of wire, shirts, pants, a dress, her underthings.

She cried out when she saw Spence's rough condition. He grinned through the cuts on his face. He had a missing tooth. She helped him out of the saddle.

"I think my ankle's busted," he said.

She noticed the dog limping too when I set it down on the ground.

"Where's Tater?" she said.

Spence shook his head.

"Dead," he said. "That's all I know."

"They killed your dog?"

"I don't know what they did, Maize. I was drunk or doped or something. All I know is I woke up on the ground, my ankle broke, Tater dead next to me, Bo limping around. Then I seen this rider with the sun behind him so I couldn't see who it was. But I knew from the way he rode in here the other day who it was and thank God for him."

"You damn fool," she said.

"I know it," he said.

She helped him limp to the house and I sauntered over to where Tom was sitting.

"How's that arm?" I asked.

"I can almost bend my fingers," he said. "Sounds like you raised a little hell out there."

I looked back the direction I'd come.

"Don't be surprised we get company tonight," I said.

"You think we will?"

"If not tonight then I think they'll leave it alone. I told them I had John Wesley Hardin out here with me. It might make them think twice."

"You think it will?"

"No."

"I couldn't swat a fly with this hand," he said.

"You're a two-gun man. If they come, kill 'em with your other hand, you need to."

His grin wasn't quite a happy one.

"Trouble is thy name, Jim," he said.

"That's very damn poetic."

"I stay around you much longer, I'll be cussing and acting like a killer."

"You know what I told 'em?"

"What?"

"That I was the Redeemer, the swift sword that would cut them down."

"Maybe that's what you are and you just don't know it. Maybe God has sent you on a mission to redeem the lives of others."

"Ha, now you *are* talking foolish. I don't know why I said it. Just mad as hell is all it was."

You could hear the deep rumble of thunder off to the north where the clouds were bunched. It would come rain soon, and maybe a whole lot more. I couldn't help but believe that a man with one eye and half his fingers missing was not going to be cowed by somebody like me. With men like him, respect and fear was everything. Maybe he'd see what I'd done as a good excuse to wipe out Spence and Maize, and maybe old Jim Glass and John Wesley Hardin too.

CHAPTER TWENTY-ONE

From the diary of Maize Walker. . .

October 1, 1885.

Whether I am in love or not with Jim Glass is yet to be known. My heart says one thing, my mind another. He is the closest to any man I've ever known to rousing in me long slumbering feelings. With him, I'd have children and they'd be beautiful and bright. But practically speaking, he is a man I suspect who disdains any thought of settlement. He told me as much.

We swam like fishes. We made love in the water and later in my bed and now it is too soon over. His eyes look to the distance. He is as eager to go wherever it is he is bound as a racehorse is anxious to start the race.

October 2, 1885.

Spence gone to town and not back yet. Unusual. Woke this morning with Jim's side of the bed yet warm. Watched him dress. His flesh pale except for his face, neck, hands, and wrists. Struck me as strange how, till I asked him, he never spoke my name. Then when he did, it sounded wonderful coming from his mouth. I do my best not to let him know how great an effect he has over me. I think he knows anyway.

He volunteered to go look for Spence and bring him home. Am worried about my brother. I am relieved Jim is going. I trust he will return with Spence in tow.

Spent the day in and out of the garden, Jim helped me with the weeding. We hoe in the pumpkin patch together. I tell him about Grandpa, the Indians. It feels natural enough—like two souls long together.

Jim says if Spence is not back by night-fall he will go look for him in the morning.

Outside I hear the sound of ax against wood. It sounds like my heart being split apart.

Jim chooses to sleep on the kitchen floor. Already my bed feels empty without him.

She sits propped up in bed, the shadows and wavering lamp's light dancing over the page as she writes. How, she wonders, did she allow herself to hope when long ago she'd given up all such hope? *Is it worse to hope than not?* Her breasts feel heavy, swollen from the wanting of his touch. She is restless without knowing why—a vague feeling that has plagued her all day.

It is time to stop writing.

She lays down her pen and stoppers the small bottle of ink and closes the diary and sets it under her pillow then turns down the wick until darkness fills the room. She closes her eyes then opens them again, staring into the blackness, then rises and goes out to where he lies near the kitchen stove on a pallet and lies down beside him, her back to his front and reaches around and takes his arm and drapes it over her. And at last she is at peace.

October 3, 1885.

Jim came home with Spence looking like he'd been dragged through the chaparral, all cut & bloody with his ankle hurt. One dog dead, one also hurt. Spence claims he can't remember how he got in such a condition. I wanted to say, "You lay down with whores and drink their whiskey, there is no telling the outcome." But instead did the best I could to repair him.

Jim expresses concern there may come trouble from Clancy and his boys after nightfall. Says we should all be ready. A world full of land and we have to fight over a small patch of it.

I ache to run off with Jim.

CHAPTER TWENTY-TWO

Dusk brought with it the anticipated rain. Tom sat at the table with his hand resting on a pillow Maize had gotten him. Spence with his foot propped on a chair, the toes purple. The dog lay in the corner, its head between its paws, eyebrows twitching whenever one of them moved or said anything. Maize fretted about getting us all supper, saying that we should eat and moving back and forth between stove and table. I stood at the window until it got too dark to see beyond the curtain of falling rain.

"I'm going to go outside for a while," I said.

I took my hat and rifle and went out and stood under the bit of overhang there at the front door —a small sheet of corrugated tin nailed to the top of two poles just there in front of the door. The rain hammered the tin like small stones. Lightning shook through the bruised sky. The darkness and rain obliterated everything between the flashes of lightning. "Maybe they wouldn't come in this weather," Tom said earlier, just as it started to rain.

I could see the destruction they'd leave behind. Four of us dead, the place burnt to a pile of smoldering gray ash that the wind would eventually carry away. In short enough time there would be nothing left to mark our having existed.

Maize came out in a little while.

"You hungry, Jim? Come on in and eat."

"I better keep watch," I said.

She looked into the uneasy darkness. The rain was gathering in puddles near our feet and it looked and sounded at times like the water was boiling up from the ground.

"You think Clancy and his men will come in this?"

"I don't guess the rain will stop them if they're looking for a fight. It wouldn't me."

I saw the look on her face when I said that, the interior light of the house falling softly on her cheeks.

"I can shoot a gun, Jim. I'm a better shot than Spence."

"That's good to know," I said. "You might just have to practice your skill."

She stood close to me and I could smell her washed hair.

"Maybe it's just as well they come," she said. "Maybe we can end the conflict between us one way or the other. It would be better in a way than just waiting all the time for them to come. I am surprised that Clancy didn't kill Spence."

"He wanted to put the last bit of fear in him," I said. "Sometimes there are worse things you can do to a man than killing him."

"Well, if they come tonight he might be sorry he let Spence live."

"You prepared for that? Is he?" I said. "To take lives?"

"It has to end sooner or later."

"I think I'm going over and wait under that tool shed," I said. "It might be better if we can catch them in a cross fire if they come."

"Tell me what to do," she said.

"Get a rifle and put out the lights and stand here in the doorway. Give Spence a gun and set him by the window. Tom will know what to do, even if he has to shoot with his off hand. You hear or see anything coming, strike a match just inside the door so I can see it but they can't. I'll do the same."

"Jim . . ."

I ducked out through the rain before she could say whatever it was she was thinking and made it across to the toolshed and stood in the door frame. The house was close enough I could see its shape even through the curtain of rain. Time would tell. The rain hammered down with fury at times, letting up, then coming hard again. The night sky vibrated with lightning, rumbled with thunder. The sound of the rain was a steady hiss like you'd imagine a roomful of demons would make.

An hour passed, then two.

Suddenly they were there, at the edge of the

property. One minute it was just the rain and darkness, then a flash of light from the storm lit them: several men sitting horses near the house. I struck a match and snapped it out. I hoped Maize saw it.

Between the lightning, you couldn't see much of anything. I aimed the rifle at where I'd seen them. Then waited. As soon as the next flash came I fired, jacked lever and fired again. They cut loose soon as I fired my first round, and so did the others inside the house. I could hear glass breaking. I could see the flashes of their guns and I unloaded into them and when the rifle went empty I pulled my pistol and emptied it too. Then almost as suddenly as it had begun, it stopped, the sound of gunfire dying in the rain. It couldn't have lasted more than a minute, two at the most—the whole fight.

The storm marched off in the distance and with it the lightning. The rest was silence. I waited. All night we waited in silence. Then the rain quit just before dawn, leaving the first morning light to shimmer on the wet dark land.

There were three dead men near the house. Two of them were facedown, their arms spread out and above their heads. The third man lay on his side facing away. I crossed to the house and went inside.

Tom and Spence were there. A trail of blood

led from the doorway to the cot they'd laid Maize on. Spence looked defeated.

"They shot her, Jim," Tom said, shaking his head.

Her eyes were partially opened and I bent and touched her cool face and closed her lids. It was like touching two small smooth stones. The bullet had struck her through the breast, leaving a drying flower of blood on her clothes.

Something heavier than anyone could describe was in the room with us. She looked like she'd simply gone to sleep. I took a blanket and pulled it over her. She looked cold and lonely and I wanted to lie beside her and hold her but it was way too late.

"Maybe you could say something," I said to Tom.

He said, "Yes . . . if Spence would like me to." He looked at Spence, who sat there with his head hanging down, his longish brown hair fallen over his face.

"She wasn't a churchgoer," he mumbled. "Neither of us were. No time for God and godly things in this godless land. But I'd be grateful if you said something if you know how."

So Tom spoke softly as though he were confiding in a friend: "Lord, take this woman's spirit into your bosom and let her there reside for all days eternal. In your kingdom she will be an angel, for she is now free of all her earthly bonds, all obligations, all regrets and pain and suffering. Amen."

Spence rubbed his eyes with the heel of his hands and looked up through his lank hair and said, "Those were nice words, Tom. I know she'd have liked them."

I rose and went outside because I didn't want to have to look at Maize in death one more minute. One of her earthly bonds had been me, and I was still tied to her in a way that any man is tied to any woman he's shared intimacy with. And that is not something so easily forgotten.

I took in a deep breath and let it out again. And then walked over to the dead lying in the quickly drying mud, the sun risen now over the mountains, its heat gaining strength.

One by one I turned them over and recognized the first two as being men I'd seen at Clancy's. The third one, the one lying on his side, was Clancy himself. I knew before I turned him over, by the stubbed fingers on the hand that lay twisted back behind him. His mouth was agape as though the bullet had caught him by surprise. I hoped to hell it was Maize's bullet that got him.

Tom helped Spence hobble out and they stood there looking at the dead men.

"Clancy," I said, standing over the body.

"Help me over there," Spence said and leaned on Tom, and when they got to the body of

Clancy, Spence spat on him and said, "You son of a bitch."

Tom and me just looked at each other. I understood Spence's grief and anger, and maybe Tom did too.

"I'll dig the graves," I said. "Is there any place special you want me to bury Maize?"

"She liked that swim hole down yonder . . ." He pointed with his chin but I already knew where it was. "Somewhere down there would be nice."

I went down with a shovel and found a spot above where the swim rock was, where you could look down onto the water, and dug a good deep grave then went and got her body and carried it down and buried her as gently as I knew how. I patted the last shovelful of dirt down with my bare hands and smoothed it out and then sat down next to her, my shirt soaked with sweat.

"You'll get to look at your swimming place every day," I said. "And, I'll remember it and you long as I live."

The wind whispered to me and I wanted to believe it was her whispering farewell even if it wasn't.

"You gave me everything, including your life, and I'm sorry Maize Walker. I'm sorry as hell."

I went up and loaded the dead men one by one onto the backs of the three horses—mine and Tom's and Spence's—and walked them all three a good distance out of sight of the house and dug one large grave. It took me a while but I finally got one dug. Maybe not deep enough to keep the coyotes and critters from catching the scent and digging them up eventually, but probably a better grave than the one they would have dug for us if the situation had been reversed.

I dragged them and dropped them in and it was onerous work and I cursed them for their stupidity at having made it so I had to do this. When I finished, I went back to the house and tied off the horses and then went down to the swim hole. I stripped naked and plunged into the cool water and looked up through it at the sunlight filtering through its greenness. I felt as though I could simply stay down under it the rest of my life and did not surface until my lungs were burning for lack of air.

I tried washing away the stink of death but it did not want to wash away completely. Tom was sitting on the warm rock when I surfaced.

"I feel terrible about what's happened," he said after I climbed out and dried myself and began to dress.

"So do I, but there's not a hell of a lot we can do about it. Everybody who is responsible for this is already dead."

"Bad karma," he said, shaking his head. He sat

with his legs drawn up, his forearms resting on his knees.

"So you mentioned once before."

Dressed now, I sat down next to him and we stared at the water and not at Maize's fresh dug grave.

"Were you in love with her?" he said.

I thought about it for a long moment.

"No, I don't believe I was. I liked her and maybe even loved her, but I wasn't *in* love with her."

"She told me something while you went to look for Spence," he said. "I am not sure I should even tell you, for it is not going to matter now. But I think it is the *right* thing I should say it."

I sat listening.

"She said she was sure she was pregnant with your child. I just thought you should know what she was thinking, what she was feeling."

I listened to the silence of the water, the quietness of sky. I wanted to tell Tom it wasn't possible for her to know such a thing with any certainty. But then a question pressed into my denial: *What if?* It was something I didn't want to consider. It felt like I'd swallowed a stone. *What happens to the dead? What happens to the person we were when the body dies? What happens to that thing inside us that causes us to love, to do with the body?*

"We need to move on soon as possible," I said. "If you still want to go, that is."

"I've given it some thought," he said.

"Well," I said, standing and brushing off the seat of my jeans. "You don't owe me anything, Tom. If anybody owes anybody it's me that owes you."

"I guess nobody is indebted to anyone here, we've all paid our debts in full."

"I'm going to walk back up to the house."

I saw him stand and look off to where I'd dug Maize's grave, the large rock I'd found for a headstone.

"You picked a good place for her, Jim."

"I think so too."

He said, "I'll walk back up to the house with you."

And the late afternoon light threw our shadows long across the rock, shadows that seemed to follow us sadly.

CHAPTER TWENTY-THREE

We started early, Tom and me, the light without the sun in it shadowy and unkempt. Tom wore his arm in a homemade sling now and could close his hand about halfway. He still couldn't grip one of his two guns. We rode steady for most of the day, the loose caliche shifting under the horses' hooves. Riding toward the rising sun, a blaze of red lifted over the lip of the earth.

We arrived in Coffin Flats the second evening.

"I want to look in on Chalk Bronson," I said. "But we ought to find you a doctor to take a look at your arm."

"You go ahead and I'll go look for a physician," he said.

"We can meet up later at the Bison—that saloon yonder," I said, pointing out the Bison Club.

He nodded. "Might be a good place to ask where the doc is," he said.

"I'll meet you there in half an hour."

I rode on down to Chalk's place, dismounted and slapped the dirt out of my clothes best I could with my Stetson before knocking.

His wife answered the door and looked at me for a long moment, then said, "Oh, it's you. Come in."

Chalk was sitting at the table with a book open in the glow of a lamp. His hands were still bandaged, but the rest of him was looking normal again, the cuts on his face now like black marks someone had drawn there with a small paintbrush.

He looked at me as though he expected to see Antonia.

"What are you doing back here?" he said.

"I wonder if we might have a private talk."

He looked at his wife.

"Go ahead and say what you have to, Nora knows everything."

"Can I get you some coffee?" she said.

"Yes, that would be nice."

I sat down across from him, the book's pages falling back from where he had it opened.

"It's about all I can do these days, read," he said. "Forgot how much I used to enjoy it."

His wife set a cup of coffee down in front of me. "You take sugar with it?" she asked.

"No ma'am."

She took a seat next to Chalk. You could see how much she loved him.

"We got off the train in Refugio," I said. "The next morning the local law came and arrested us." I saw the worry come into his face.

"For what reason?"

"Because the lawman there happens to be a cousin or some such to Johnny Waco."

Chalk nodded. "He telegraphed ahead."

"Yeah."

"What about Antonia?"

"They took her. Escorted her back to Waco's. I think that's where she is now, with him."

"So it all went for nothing?"

"Yeah, pretty much."

"They just let you go?"

"In a manner of speaking," I said. "But not without a proper sendoff."

"Can you pour us something a little stronger

240

than the coffee, love?" he said to her.

She rose from the table and went to a cupboard and got down a bottle of liquor and three glasses. He looked at her when she poured some in all three.

"Nora, when did you start drinking?" he said.

"I guess when you decided to go save your ex-wife and get yourself near killed for your trouble," she told him.

We all three drank down what she'd poured. I don't know it made any of us feel any better, but it probably didn't make us feel worse.

"Now what?" he said.

"I'm going to go get her."

"Let it go, Jim. You did what you could, it didn't work out. Next time he'll kill you."

"You know, Chalk, I would do that very thing, just let it go. Except I can't. It's just not in me to do so."

"I can't help you no more, Jim. I can't help Antonia no more. I've got Nora to think about. And these hands of mine ain't never going to heal right and I don't know if I'll ever be able to use them for anything. I already paid all the price I can afford."

He looked broken in more than just his hands.

"I'm not asking you to do anything more," I said. "I just came to see how you were making out."

She poured us another glass each of the liquor

and we sat and drank like three old friends even though we didn't know very much about each other except we were all bonded by the same thing: injustice.

"All I ever wanted in life was just to be a footloose puncher," I said to neither of them in particular. "And I was fairly well content with my life till all this happened. I'd like for things to go back to what they were, and maybe they will eventually . . ."

"Some things happen that change us forever, Jim," he said, looking down at his hands.

"You're right, they do," I said, and stood. "Take care of yourself, Chalk."

"You as well, Jim."

His wife looked at me as though she was glad I was leaving. I didn't blame her.

The night air breathed a cool wind and I walked over to the Bison and went inside where men tended to their needs and commiserated with their own brand of misery, lives not all lived in the way they'd hoped, just as my own wasn't lived in a way I'd once dreamt of. They stood along the bar and gathered around the few tables. Bill was there at his usual spot behind the bar. I did not yet see Tom.

I walked to the bar and took up residence near the far end and Bill came down and said, "I never thought I'd see you 'round these parts again. I heard you ran off with Johnny Waco's woman, stole her after you delivered her up there from Pink's hog farm . . ."

"You just here to ask questions or do you still sell beer in this place?" I said, ignoring the comment.

He moved down and pulled a tap till he filled a beer glass then walked it back and set it in front of me. "Takes some balls to show back up around here." It was a caution not a threat. "They'll be looking for you they hear you're back in town."

"I'm supposed to meet a friend of mine here, fellow with his arm in a sling. You seen him?"

"He was in a little while ago looking for a doc. I sent him over to Doc Flax's place."

I drank my beer and watched four men at a table playing poker, listened to them grouse and tell jokes and lose money and win it. They were playing for low stakes, no more than a fifty cent limit. They weren't the sort of men who would play for big money, just cattlemen and punchers looking to lose themselves from wives who were waiting home, or to avoid empty cots in a bunk-house somewhere.

I paid for my beer and told Bill that if my friend returned to tell him to wait for me and walked out again into the black night and looked to the far side of the tracks were a few lanterns were hung in the doorways and windows. A locomotive stood on the tracks, behind it a line of passenger cars, quiet and dark as a dead beast waiting the morning run.

I walked across the dead line and reached Pink's place. Inside I could hear a man's laughter, and then a woman's. I knocked on the door and Lorri answered.

"Well, my my," she said with a smile. I could see she was a little drunk. A fancy dude was sitting there on the horsehair divan across from the pimp, Pink Huston. They were passing a crystal decanter of what looked like some expensive whiskey back and forth.

Pink looked toward the door and said, "Who is it?"

"An old friend of ours," Lorri said and stepped back to let me in.

"The pugilist," he said. It sounded more like a cuss word than a compliment. "You bring Antonia back to me?"

The other man had thin graying hair combed over from a part just above his left ear. His face was red. His shoes were soft and black and polished. He was heavy as a grass fed heifer.

"I'd come to see if she maybe had made her way back here to you," I said.

"Can I get you something, cowboy?" Lorri said. She was standing with her back to Pink and I could see the look in her eyes held the promise of more than just a drink if I wanted it and was willing to play a game of deception.

"I just came to see about Antonia," I said. It gave me a little satisfaction to say that to her, as though she and I were playing a game that only the two of us knew the rules to.

"Oh, is that all?"

"She ain't here, and the way I see it, you owe me for her services unrendered," Pink said. He started to stand, I guess to make himself look tough in front of his friend, maybe in front of Lorri too.

"You a slaver?" I said.

That stopped him short, that and the fact he'd had too much to drink and was unsteady. He fell back down.

"Slaver?"

"The last I heard people were free to go where they wanted. Unless of course you're a slaver, which would make you something illegal."

The other man was eyeing me with mild curiosity, maybe waiting for something bad to happen between me and Pink, a bloodletting perhaps.

"T'fuck ya want here! Git him the hell out," he shouted at Lorri.

She took me by the elbow and guided me to the door, stepped outside with me, pulling her red silken robe tight to her against the cool night air.

"Why don't you come back later, after Pink's passed out. No sense in all of us having a lousy night," she said.

"You know, if it were a different time and I was in a different mood, I'd probably take you up on that offer," I said. She reached down and took my hand and placed it inside the robe.

"You sure about that?" she said.

She was warm and soft and round where my hand touched, like a dream you want to fall into on a cold night. I let it linger there for a second then withdrew it.

"Oh, that it were so simple," I said, and turned and walked away.

"Oh, but it is," I heard her say.

I walked back up to the Bison and Tom was there. Standing alone, looking out of place.

"How'd you make out at the doc's?" I said.

He looked down at his arm.

"He said I was on the mend and there wasn't much more he could do for me than what had already been done. He gave me these pills . ." He reached in his pocket and took out a small envelope. "For the pain. I took one and now I'm feeling sort of okay."

"Cocaine pills," I said.

"Really?"

"They'll do the trick."

"So I'm finding out. How about you, you see your friend?"

"Yeah."

I ordered us a beer then said, "You drink beer, don't you?"

"Sure, why not? I'm a two-gun killer and a doper now. What harm's a little glass of beer?"

We drank slowly.

"What's your plan?" he said. "You got one yet?"

"I'm working on it."

He flexed the fingers on his bad hand.

"They don't hurt so bad," he said. "Nothing does."

"That's why people like those pills," I said.

We sipped our beer.

I didn't notice the four punchers that came in until Bill eased down to our end of the bar and said, "Those boys that just came in—down the other end of the bar—those are some of Waco's boys."

They were hard-looking men in long coats and chaps with their hat brims set down low over their eyes, and they stood at the end of the bar without talking, just drinking their beer.

"They see you here they'll run back and tell Johnny and he'll come with even more of 'em and probably tie you to a horse and drag you till you're nothing but raw meat and rags."

"When'd you start to worry about guys like me?" I said.

"Ain't you I'm worried for, I just don't want my place tore up he finds you here."

I looked at Tom and he looked at me.

"They look like working boys to me," I said.

"Waco pays 'em regular if that's what you mean," Bill said. "But he pays 'em for whatever he wants done and not just running his cows and mending fence."

"Yeah, well, I guess we'll have to see," I said.

Tom slipped his revolver out with his good hand and held it just inside his duster and said, "Go ahead, I'm right behind you."

He followed me down to where they stood drinking and I said, "You're off Johnny Waco's outfit?"

They turned their heads to look at me and Tom.

"I'm not looking for a fight with you boys," I said. "I just wanted to know if he got his wife back all right."

The one, a knotty fellow you could see had some bulk to him, gave me a hard stare.

"What business would that be of yours?"

Before I could answer him another one, a tall hook-nosed, sandy-haired puncher said, "That's the old boy was with Chalk that day, you remember, Hank?"

The knotty one rubbed his chin.

A smile parted his rough beard.

"I'm a mother's son," he said. "You run off with ol' John's woman then bring your sorry ass back here. Mister, you must have a death wish."

"No," I said. "I just came back to see if she got home again safe and sound."

"Goddamn," another one said. "You believing this?"

They all four grew grins.

"Maybe we ought to truss him up and take him back with us as a early Christmas present. Ol' John would probably put something extra in our stockings."

They were laughing but you could feel the tension.

"It's just a simple question," I said. "Is she out there with him now?"

The knotty one shoved me away suddenly, nearly causing me to lose my balance, which only added to their perverse humor.

"Tell you what," he said. "Git on your goddamn nag and ride clear out of the territory and we'll forget we even seen you. And take that lame arm sissy standing there with you."

"Yeah, you're probably right," I said. "I should do that."

Then I hit him so hard I couldn't tell for a moment whether it was my hand that shattered or his skull. And when the other three started to make their play, Tom brought out his gun and said, "I got enough pills in this to give you two each. Sleeping pills, and death is a long sleep. My friend asked you a civil question and he'd like an answer."

They looked from the barrel of Tom's fancy pistol down to their friend who lay cold as stone at their feet. His head had struck a spittoon and turned it over onto himself so that along with the blood there was the stain of tobacco juice and old chewed plugs and wet cigar stubs.

"She's out there," the hook nose said. "I don't see where that's no business of your'n."

I stepped over the one I hit and said to the three, "You boys don't know how close you come to dying tonight. That one there," I nodded toward Tom, "is John Wesley Hardin, and most generally when he pulls his piece somebody ends up dusted." I don't know if they believed one damn word but at this point Tom and me had gotten the upper hand on them and the answer I'd wanted and that was enough.

We watched them pick up their smashed friend and carry him by the arms out the door, presumably on their way back to Johnny Waco's to tell their tale, which was exactly what I wanted. If I knew anything at all about Antonia, she was a woman who could read a plan even if it wasn't completely spelled out for her.

We walked out after the punchers rode off and stood there in the night air.

Tom said, "You're going to get me killed, aren't you?"

"I'm going to try my best not to. That's why this is where we part company, my friend."

"You're going to try and do this alone?"

"Look, two against all them or one against all

250

them, it isn't going to matter. We're too few in number, me and you, Tom. Even if you *were* John Wesley Hardin it wouldn't matter. Waco will send as many men as he needs to. I can't outfight them all and I don't plan to. People don't live as long as we do because we're tough, we live as long as we do because we're just a tad smarter than the other guy. At least I'd like to believe that."

"Okay," he said.

"Let's get us some rooms and then you head out first thing tomorrow in case they come early."

He nodded. Somewhere a dog barked. Somebody laughed from inside the saloon. Lights from across the tracks beckoned the lonely. The town was heading toward sleep.

CHAPTER TWENTY-FOUR

She held the bottle of mercury in her hands, the one she'd gotten Pedro to get her the last time he'd gone to town. For days she'd been struggling with the decision: life, or death?

Maria, had, if anything, become more cruel toward her, had chided her at every opportunity, and she'd had no will to fight back. The only one who showed her the least bit of kindness was the old man, Maria's henpecked husband, Pedro.

On the day she'd asked him to buy her the mercury, he'd been grooming one of Johnny Waco's favorite horses, a tall roan with a coat like polished mahogany.

She could tell that Pedro felt a kinship to the animals, for he spoke to them lovingly whenever he groomed them.

When she pressed the money into his hand and asked him to buy her the mercury, he tried to refuse.

"*Por favor, no pida el de mí,* missus."

"You're the only one I can ask such a favor of, Pedro."

He acted at first as if he hadn't heard her, ran his brush down over the haunches of the big horse until she stopped him by touching his wrist.

"Please," she said.

He nodded finally and took the money and had brought the bottle under his serape when he returned from town and gave it to her with the saddest eyes.

"What will you do with it?" he asked her, though he was pretty sure he already knew, for he'd seen a prostitute in Nogales drink it when he was a young border outlaw, before he took a bullet to the hip and gave up his wild ways. In death her lips and flesh were as blue as winter ice.

"*Está de ninguna consecuencia,*" she said. It's of no consequence.

He crossed himself, though he was no longer sure if God paid any attention to him because of all the bad things he'd done in his youth. And he was sure that as part of his punishment, God had given him Maria, who, among her other distasteful actions, had lately taken to sneaking up to the *jefe*'s house late at night. His Maria had turned him into something less than a man. It was only the *jefe*'s wife, Antonia, who treated him with respect. But he knew he had to be careful and not show her too much attention or deference, or Señor Waco would do to him what he'd done to the gringo lawman.

Still, he liked her and was willing to take some risk, just as he had done when she'd asked him to get her a gun the last time she ran away. It was a pity to see her brought back by an armed man and handed over once more to Señor Waco; if anything, Antonia looked even more pitiful and sad than she had before she ran away.

Every night in their bed, when she had not snuck off to the big house, his wife complained to him about Antonia. "That woman!" she called her. "She's no good for Mr. Waco," she would say. "He needs a good woman, not some *puta* who will run off the minute he turns his back."

He told her to hush her harsh talk, which only incited her all the more. He had come to conclude there was no use arguing with his wife, that he had no more power over her than he had over anything else. His time had come and gone with the coming and going of his youth. Old age had left him a man simply waiting for the end to come and to take him to whatever heaven or hell awaited men like him. He had thought when he married such a younger woman it would somehow return to him at least a little of his youth, but instead it had done the opposite, made him feel even older and more useless.

It gave him a good feeling to help the woman, even if it *was* to kill herself, he thought when he'd handed over the bottle of mercury. At least he would help her escape whatever misery she was in. *Such beauty, such a waste. If only I were a young bandit again, I would steal her away for myself.*

She heard the commotion downstairs and went to the door and listened. Some of Johnny's hands had come in talking loud, telling him, "That fellow was with Chalk that day—the one who stole your wife, Mr. Waco—well, we by God run into him at the Bison Club. He was in there bold as brass."

Another of them said, "He hit Rolle straight in the mouth, knocked him cold as the bottom of a well. Show him where your tooth is missing, Rolle."

Her heart raced a little. *Was it even possible Jim had come back for her?*

"He had to know we'd come tell you, Mr.

Waco. You know if we'd been armed we'd taken care o' him for you, don't you, Mr. Waco?"

"You get some of the boys, a dozen or so, and have them ready to leave here first light. Tell them I want them armed, pistols and rifles."

"Yes sir," they said. She heard them shuffle out and went to the window and saw their shadows crossing the ground toward the bunk-house.

She heard him call her name.

"Antonia!"

She did not answer. She heard his heavy steps ascending the stairs.

"Antonia," he said again as he approached her closed door. She slipped the bottle of mercury under a satin-covered pillow there on her bed.

He opened the door and stood there.

"I guess you heard," he said.

She feigned ignorance.

"He's back and I aim to kill him. I'm tired of this goddamn business."

She looked at him without trying to hide her hatred.

"If I have to kill every man in the territory who would have you or who you'd go off with, then that is what I'll do. And if need be, I'll kill you as well."

She pulled at the bodice of her dress so that her flesh was exposed, the upper swell of her breasts.

"Shoot me right here—through my heart," she said. "Why not do it and end it and go and live with that Mexican wench and then you both can be as miserable as I've been."

He took one step into the room. She remained defiant.

"Do it, John."

He turned suddenly and left, closing the door behind him.

She quickly went to the window and saw the lights still on in the small adobe—Pedro and Maria's quarters just off the west corner of the house. She stood watching until the door opened and Maria emerged and then closed the door behind her, then watched as she went around back of the main house. Satisfied that Maria and Johnny would be occupied for some little while there at the back of the house in one of the spare rooms, she then slipped down the front stairs, pausing only long enough to take money from the safe and to write something on a piece of paper that she wrapped the money in, then went down to the adobe.

Pedro had a rope in his hand he'd been weaving.

"I need you to go and find the man named Jim Glass and tell him to meet me at the grove as soon as he can come."

"No, señora, I cannot go. Señor Waco will fire me, or worse . . ."

"*El consiste en allí coger a su esposa, Pedro* —your wife and Señor Waco, right this moment."

The old man dropped his eyes in shame.

"I know what they are doing, señora."

"Take a horse and this money and go home," she said. "After you've found Mr. Glass, go back to your home in Mexico."

He looked at it. She'd never seen such sorrow in a man's face.

"Take his best horse and the saddle," she said. "This is a bill of sale for it. No one will question you as the owner."

He looked on the verge of tears.

"I will do it," he said, "if you do something for me."

"Anything."

"Let me kiss you."

She saw in his eyes that it wasn't so much desire as it was loneliness and drew his face to hers with both hands and gently kissed him on the mouth.

"It is enough," he said when she pulled back. "*Gracias . . .*"

"Hurry," she said.

"Maria will tell Mr. Waco that I've gone as soon as she returns and finds me missing."

"Write her a quick note telling her that your heart is broken because she is being unfaithful to you and that you can't take it anymore and that you are going home to Mexico. They will believe it."

He smiled. "You're very devious for someone so young," he said.

"I'm a woman," she said. "All women are devious." It was of course a veiled reference to his own wife and he knew it and smiled sadly.

"Si, all women are so."

She hurried back to her room and stood by the window and watched until she saw him come out of the adobe again and head for the corral. Then she saw the shadow of him astride the horse, the glint of silver from the saddle in the moonlight, and smiled. In a short time, she told herself, she would be free—one way or the other—and set about making her plan of escape.

And as Pedro rode away to the town on his good horse and fancy saddle, his pocket full of more money than he'd seen since a bank he'd robbed near Paso Robles and his old revolver stuck down in his belt, he felt again vital—like in the old days—and once more felt the wind against his face and the blood of a bandit rushing through his veins.

CHAPTER TWENTY-FIVE

I was already awake and dressed when the knock on my door came. The light outside was still struggling against the fading darkness—dawn against night. I opened it and found an old man standing there—Mexican under a big frayed sombrero, face as cracked and brown as old leather. His shirt was buttoned at the throat and his eyes held secrets I'd not want to know about. His ears stuck out like jug handles.

"Señor Glass?"

"Yes."

"She say to meet her in the grove soon as you can."

"Antonia?"

He nodded. "Si."

"That's what she told you?"

He nodded. "You better hurry. Señor Waco is coming soon to get you."

"How many men?"

He shrugged. "Many," he said. "More than you."

I considered for a moment it was a setup. But looking into that ancient face, I didn't see anything dishonest, just a face that had seen its share of troubles and hardship.

"What's your name?" I said.

"Pedro Montero," he said proudly. "I used to be a pretty bad hombre in my day." Then he grinned a mouthful of butternut yellow teeth and I didn't have any reason not to believe him.

"You know they might kill you for telling me these things," I said.

"Shit," he said. "They'll have to catch me first . . ." Then he turned and walked stiffly down the hall then down the stairs. I went to the window and looked down onto the street and saw him mount a good-looking animal with a saddle that had silver ingots inlaid in the pommel and wondered how a broke-down old Mexican could afford such finery. But then, like he said, he used to be a pretty tough hombre in the old days, and maybe he still was.

I pulled on my coat and hat and went down and out the front door and down the street to the livery where I'd boarded my horse. I gave the man three dollars for its keep and asked him to saddle it for me. I knew if Waco and his boys were coming, he was already on his way. I'd have to find a different route out to the ranch in order to avoid passing them on the road. I walked up to Chalk's place and knocked on the door and this time it was Chalk himself who answered even with his damaged hands.

"I'm learning to do things I used to take for

granted," he said, standing there. "Like opening the damn door."

I told him the situation.

"They might burn the town," he said.

"No, I don't think so. Some old Mexican brought me a message from Antonia. I'm to meet her in the grove again."

"You sure he's not setting you up?"

"Could be, but the old man seemed honest enough."

"Pedro," he said. "He's worked for Waco long as I can remember."

"I think he was doing her bidding."

"I can't help you, Jim. You're smart, you'll ride away from this and not look back."

"Tell me if there is a different way I can reach the ranch other than the road."

"You could swing wide west, go up through Dead Horse Canyon then cross Bitch Creek and come into the ranch from the north."

He called his wife and told her to draw a map as he gave her instructions. She didn't seem very happy I had returned but set at the table and drew the map as he described it on the back of a piece of butcher's paper and gave it to me.

"Thanks," I said. "I might not ever see you again, Chalk. Either Antonia and I will get away or they'll kill us both."

"You take care," he said. "I wish there was more I could do."

I went back down the street to the livery and Tom was there with his horse saddled.

"You heading out too?" I said.

He nodded.

"Good luck to you, Tom." I held out my hand.

"I guess I'm not ready yet to quit," he said.

"Quit what?"

"Whatever it was we were doing before."

"We weren't doing anything before."

"Yes, we had set out to save the woman," he said. "That's what it was."

"You don't want to go no farther with me, Tom. This is getting into some serious business. Waco and his men are on their way here now."

"Then we better get going," he said.

"No."

"I can't believe you're going to argue with John Wesley Hardin," he said. "Why I've shot men for less."

I shook my head and mounted up and rode off in the direction Chalk had said but Tom wouldn't quit following me and after a time I just let it go. If he aimed to get himself killed, there wasn't anything I could do about it.

We reached the canyon about noon and rode down into it and the red rock walls rose on both sides of us a good hundred feet or so and the echoes of our horse's iron shoes rang off the loose rock in a way that sounded like there were more than just two of us.

"Beautiful, isn't it?" Tom said, looking up at the walls. "Reminds us of what small and sometimes insignificant creatures we humans are . . ."

I didn't say anything; for me, it wasn't an adventure or some sort of picnic we were on and the beauty of the land had to it an unforgiving nature and could be just as cruel as any human as far as I was concerned. I felt closed in and kept wondering if Waco and his men had for some reason decided to come into Coffin Flats this same route instead of the road. But then, why would they? I didn't know, but it was in my mind a possibility. And if we encountered them in the canyon, me and Tom wouldn't stand any more chance than a block of ice in hell.

We came out of the canyon just as the sun was setting low, and there ahead of us, twinkling with that last bit of sun, was what had to be Bitch Creek, the sun on it causing it to light like it was on fire.

We crossed it and as the water came up to our stirrups I told Tom to hold his feet high unless he wanted wet boots and he said, "I'm already there," and we rode on across like that, our feet high.

Once on the far side, we let the horses have a blow and chewed on some jerky.

"What's the plan when we find her?" Tom said.

"To get the hell out of the country as quick as

we can and leave as few tracks as possible."

"Which direction?"

"Texas, I'm thinking. The Panhandle possibly. Big country, easy enough to get lost in it."

He nodded.

We tightened the cinches and got on board and rode on swinging slightly northeast this time, calculating we were already on the ranchland and just needed to locate the grove.

Dusk drew in around us like a curtain of purple. We found ourselves sitting atop a bluff looking down to some distant lights winking in a wide valley.

"That's it," I said. "That's Johnny Waco's place."

"So while we're here looking for his wife, he's in Coffin Flats looking for you?"

"From what the old man said, yes."

"Where exactly are we supposed to hook up with her, and how?"

"She'll meet us in a grove beyond those hills," I said.

"I think the Spanish word is *bosque*," he said.

"There anything you don't know?"

"Plenty, and I'm still learning."

"Well, let's go see if we can find that *bosque* in the dark then."

"Let's."

Once I got my bearings straight we eventually saw the shadows of the grove standing against the night sky. We drew reins and I gave a sharp whistle. We sat there listening. Finally we heard the footfall of a horse.

"Jim?"

"Over here," I called.

She came toward us slowly. Having a full moon helped matters. We heeled our mounts to meet her.

"Who's this?" she asked when we drew up together.

"His name is Tom, he's a friend."

"Tom Twist, ma'am."

"Johnny rode out with a dozen or so men this morning," she said. "He's looking for you in Coffin Flats."

"I know."

"I wasn't sure if Pedro would find you or just keep riding."

"He found me."

"Thank God."

"You set to go?" I said.

"Ready."

"I'm thinking we'll make a run for the border —Texas. I still got some old contacts over there I can trust. It's a good place to get lost in."

It was then that a voice shouted.

"Don't move or we'll cut you down like grass."

We whirled our animals around and saw them there astride their horses in a moonlit meadow maybe a hundred yards away.

"Ride into those woods," I said, and slapped

her horse, and me and Tom were right behind her. Gunfire erupted and you could hear the whine of bullets as they went past our heads, could hear them snapping limbs and busting against the trunks of the trees.

Tom's horse got shot from under him and I raced up fast and offered him my hand and he took it with his good hand and swung up behind me. I heard him groan as he did. We got just to the edge of the woods and my horse got shot and we both went tumbling.

Antonia's scream cut through the racket of gunfire. I pulled Tom to his feet and we found her just inside the woods trying to control her frightened animal. I told her to dismount and took the reins and forced the animal to the ground using a technique an old vaquero once taught me.

"He knew I'd come here," she said breathlessly.

"You hurt?" I asked.

"No. A bullet passed right through my blouse and I thought I'd been shot. But I'm not."

"Tom, what about you?" I said. The bullets came in through the woods like angry hornets.

"I think I broke my arm in the fall," he said through gritted teeth.

"Which one?"

"Guess."

"That arm is a curse," I said. "You might be better just cutting it off."

"I'm beginning to think so."

"How about we do some firing back," I said.

"I dropped my guns," Tom said, reaching around for them.

My own rifle was still in its scabbard.

"You two wait here," I said and began to crawl back out again, feeling along the ground as I went. I found one of Tom's pistols and grabbed it and stuck it in my belt then crawled on till I got to my own shot horse and jerked the Winchester free of the scabbard and began to lay down a field of fire at the muzzle flashes coming from Waco's men. They looked like large fireflies in the darkness. Knowing they'd quickly pick up where I was firing from, I crawled back into the woods.

"We can't stay here forever," I said.

"You two go," Antonia said. "He wants me. I'll go to him."

"No," I said.

"It's the only way you and your friend stand a chance."

"I think he's pissed off enough to kill us no matter what you do."

"Maybe, but he'll surely kill you if you don't run."

The gunfire stopped suddenly. We all took a deep breath.

"What's he planning?" Tom said.

"Who knows?"

267

"I'll give you about five minutes to come out —then I'll set those woods afire with you in them."

Antonia said it was Waco shouting the command.

Before I could stop her, she cried, "I'll come to you, Johnny, if you let them go!"

"Sure," he called back. "Why wouldn't I? What the hell I want with them?"

"Even I know a damn lie when I hear one," Tom said quietly.

"You glad you came now?" I said.

He didn't say anything.

"This is stupid," she said. "I won't let you die because of me."

"You two take out of here on your horse," I said to them. "I'll hold them off long as I can."

"No," she said.

"Tom don't deserve this," I said. "Neither do you. Get the hell out of here while the getting's to be had."

Tom said he wouldn't go either.

"Goddamn it, go!"

"What difference will it make?" she said. "He'll just find us and kill us anyway."

"He can't track you in the dark and by morning maybe you'll have found a place to hide. Take Tom and get in the wind."

Tom refused to go until I cocked the hammer of my pistol and put it against his head. "Either they'll kill you or I will," I said. "Get the fuck out of here, both of you!"

They got the horse to its feet and mounted double and I laid down more fire to hide the sound of their leaving and Waco's boys returned my fire with equal measure and I figured this was it—this was how I was going to die—just like those soldiers in the old battles when I was nothing more than a snotnose kid in a bad war —shot or burned to death, or both, in a wood without any name.

I emptied my guns then settled in and waited.

Something calm came over me.

I stopped fearing death altogether in those next few moments.

I could hear them coming.

CHAPTER TWENTY-SIX

They rode swiftly through the night of moonlit landscape. Tom could see the shape of things and it was like riding through a dream as he clung with his good arm around the woman's waist. She was a skilled rider. They rode wordlessly and there was just the sound of the horse's labored breathing, the ring of its shoes on rock and the thud of them in the soft soil, the creak of saddle leather, the whisper of wind.

They rode until the woman pulled reins and said they needed to give the horse a rest, then stood together in the moonlight looking back at the direction they'd come from. They stood quietly and listened, thinking they'd hear the rumble of other riders pursuing them. But there was just the great empty silence.

"We shouldn't have left him," Tom said softly.

"It's what he wanted," she said. "You must be good friends . ."

"No," Tom said. "We hardly know each other."

The night air was cool against their skin and she buttoned her coat around her and he said, "Are you all right?"

"Yes, I think so."

"May I ask what it was between you that made him so determined to find you?" Tom said.

She shrugged. "Nothing," she said. "Money? I don't know what else it could be. Maybe he's just one of those damn fool men who once they take on a job want to see it through."

The horse cropped bunch grass. It was like they were two lovers out for a midnight ride.

The moon stood balanced on the jagged teeth of a mountain range.

"Hunter's moon," he said, looking at it.

They mounted again and this time she rode the horse at a trot rather than a gallop, trying to preserve its stamina.

"I know of a cave not far from here," she said.

He could feel the strands of her hair against his face; they were like silk threads.

The cave was covered in brush at the foot of a smooth rock wall that had been carved and shaped by a million years of wind and rain, the same rock he'd seen earlier in the day in the canyon, beautiful if foreboding.

He helped her clear away the brush enough so they could enter and bring the horse in with them.

"We'll need a fire," she said, and together they gathered some of the brush that lay along the slope of the ground leading to the cave and dragged it inside then recovered the entrance once they'd got a fire started. The floor of the cave was sand with scattered small rocks and clay chips she said were from the days when the ancient people lived in this cave. "It's shards of their pots and dishes," she said.

"I know," he said.

"You've been in these caves before?"

"No. But I have read about these people."

She unsaddled the horse and it stood out of the fire's light, sleeping on its feet, weary from the weight of two riders, the pace.

The light danced along the cave's ceiling, which was several feet taller than Tom when he stood.

"I brought a little food," she said, reaching into the saddlebags she'd placed next to the saddle. She retrieved a large wedge of cheese and some crackers, a bottle of whiskey and one of wine. He took notice.

"How's your arm?" she said.

"I'd just as soon I didn't own it."

They ate measuredly, taking small bits of the cheese and crackers. She said, "Do you prefer wine or the harder stuff?"

"Wine," he said.

She handed the bottle to him and he watched as she took the cork from the whiskey and tipped it to her mouth. She did not drink indelicately, but he thought she was someone who wasn't tasting whiskey for the first time. He noticed too the way her hands shook.

"What causes that?" he said.

"Causes what?"

"Your hands to shake the way they are."

She looked at them then took another drink of the whiskey.

"I'm just cold," she said.

"Not some other reason, afraid maybe?"

"No," she said. "Just cold."

Later she lay with the saddle blanket over her, her head resting on the saddle, the bottle cradled in the crook of her arm; she'd drank nearly half. He knew then what caused her hands to shake.

He sat with his knees pulled up, feeding the fire when it needed it. Inside the cave it was pure silence except for the sound of water dripping somewhere deeper, a rhythmic steady sound. He did his best to ease the pain of his broken arm; he didn't think it was broken badly, a small bone somewhere in the forearm, he guessed it to be. Just added misery to the healing snakebite. He closed his eyes and tried not to think of the sharp little stabs of pain that came and went. His weariness overcame him.

He awoke to the darkness and saw needle points of light penetrating the brush covering the entryway. The woman was yet asleep and he took the half-empty bottle from her and replaced it in her saddlebags then shook her shoulder till she came awake.

"God," she moaned, cupping her head in her hands. "I always forget what whiskey does to me—not like opium at all . . ."

Then realizing what she'd said, she tried making a joke of it.

"It's okay," he said. "I understand."

She looked into his eyes and saw something she hadn't seen in a man's eyes since she saw it in those of Chalk Bronson's.

"We better get the hell out of here," she said, and rose and took the saddle blanket and saddle and swung it up on the horse's back and tightened the cinch while he went to the entrance and tried to see out through the brush pile.

"What's it look like?" she said over her shoulder as she made the final loop of the cinch strap.

"Looks clear," he said.

"How's your arm?"

He looked down at it, his fingers cold and stiff, but he could flex his hand at the wrist without too much pain.

"It's good," he said.

She came over and said, "Let me see." He held it to the light coming through the brush. Her fingers felt his.

"This hurt?"

"No."

"How about this?"

"Yes, a little."

They were standing inches apart and he could feel something tense between the two of them and he wasn't sure what it was—his imagination or something other.

Her fingers lingered a moment longer there along his wrist.

"I thought at one time I wanted to be a nurse," she said. "I don't know why I never did anything more with my life than I have . . ."

"You're still young enough yet to do things you want," he said.

Her gaze lowered from his.

"We should try and find you a doctor soon as possible," she said. He looked down at her lingering fingers; there was nothing unusual about them except for the way they felt against his pain.

She turned then and went and took the horse's reins while he pushed aside the brush enough so she could lead the animal out. The sun had not yet risen above the red rocks, and the sky was colorless at that hour. Somewhere in the chaparral they could hear quail dusting themselves and cooing. She swung up into the saddle and kicked a foot free from the stirrup so he could swing up behind her. She waited until he put his good arm around her waist. She felt somehow safe with it there.

For him, the feeling of holding to her was different somehow this morning than it had been last night. They were pressed together in a way that was comforting to each of them. It seemed to him like she waited a long time before heeling the horse into a lope, but it had only been a moment in their lives.

CHAPTER TWENTY-SEVEN

I'd heard rumors that the last of Custer's men shot each other to prevent their enemies from capturing them, knowing as they must the results if taken alive. Whether or not it was true, I could understand men in dire straits doing that very thing. I'd half considered saving my last bullet for me, knowing as I did what Waco would have done to me by his drovers.

But when it came right down to it, I'd rather have spent that last bullet in the hopes it would blow up one of their hearts than to take my own life with it. Something about shooting myself seemed cowardly, or maybe it was just the opposite—maybe it was too brave a thing.

I sat there like I was waiting for them when they found me. They leveled their guns and I figured it was execution time until Waco said, "Don't kill him, not yet anyway.

"Where are they?" he said.

"Gone," I said. "Fled. Left me here to die, the dirty bastards." I said it with a smile.

"Where'd they go, goddamn it!"

"Big country," I said. "Your guess is as good as mine."

"And you just what, stayed behind to be the hero?"

"I would have gone with them," I said, "but we flipped a coin and I lost."

"Get him on his feet, boys."

Two of them yanked me to a standing position and Waco backhanded me hard, but I'd been hit harder.

"You *will* tell me," he said.

I spat out a mouthful of blood.

"Probably not, since I don't know any more than you do where they're at. They say ignorance is bliss."

"Who's the other one who was with you?" he asked.

"John Wesley Hardin."

He backhanded me again and my ears rang.

"Can't get blood out of a turnip," I said.

"Yeah, you're right, but I sure as hell can get it out of you."

He hit me again, this time with his closed fist, and it would have dropped me to my knees except for the two holding me up.

"Take him back to the house and lock him in the smoke shed," Waco ordered. "We can't track them tonight but we'll head out first thing in the morning. Harker, go find the Indian and bring him."

I was tied at the wrists and a rope was dropped over me and cinched around my middle by some chap-wearing waddie who dallied the other end of his lariat round his saddle horn. He said, "You best keep up, or this is going to hurt."

Then he spurred his horse into a trot and of course I ran for about twenty paces before I stumbled over a rock I couldn't see in that nightglow of moonlight and fell and that waddle was true to his word about it hurting, being dragged through the chaparral like that.

Time we reached the ranch I was feeling

about half dead and almost wished I was because being bounced over that rough ground like that wasn't anything you'd want to do twice. He dismounted and let the rope go slack and a couple of others came up and lifted me and half carried me to the smokehouse and locked me in it. I by God didn't do much but try and not think how bad off I felt over every inch of my body. Hadn't been for that canvas coat of mine and those tough Levi's, I wouldn't have been fit to feed to the dogs.

I wondered why Waco didn't just have me killed instead of going to all this trouble. But it was late and I was too tired and hurting to care. At that point killing me would have been doing me a favor. I closed my eyes. I'd made my peace.

The door rattled open and morning light came in so sharp it hurt my eyes and two of Waco's men dragged me out by the arms and dropped me at the feet of a few dozen horses upon one of which sat Johnny Waco in a big sheepskin coat.

The morning was cool and bright as polished steel. Next to Waco sat a dark-skinned man I guessed to be the Indian. He sat staring balefully down at me the way you might look at horse apples.

"It's not over yet, if that's what you're thinking," Waco said. Then to the boys on either side of me: "Get him on a horse."

I didn't figure they were going to go through

all the trouble of riding me out a ways just to kill me, that there was some purpose to his madness. But I was damned if I knew what it was.

We rode to the grove again and the Indian began to cut sign and we rode on through the grove and out the other side and I looked but couldn't see how the Indian could cut sign when nothing seemed visible. But he did and we rode in a due westerly fashion, down the slope of a ridge and across what I guessed was still part of Bitch Creek and out the other side. We halted while the Indian rode up and down then waved us on. I counted nearly thirty riders and I didn't know why he needed so many other than to make sure there was nothing left to chance. Waco rode out in front of his crew but behind the lead of the Indian.

That Indian tracked over hard rock and how he did it was anybody's guess, but Waco seemed to have full faith in him and by mid-morning we reached a rock wall with lots of brush blown up at its base. The Indian pointed and Waco pulled his gun and ordered some of the drovers, "Go see what that fucking Indian is pointing at."

Several of them rode forward and dismounted and turned and one of them said, "We don't see nothing what he's pointing at, boss."

Waco looked at the Indian again and he heeled his horse forward and leaned and pulled away a chunk of brush and there was a hole in the wall.

It proved to be a cave but there wasn't anyone in it.

"Looks like they may have camped the night, or somebody did," one of the drovers said, coming out again and brushing gray ash from his hands.

Waco looked at the Indian, and he rode up and down cutting sign and it didn't take him long before he started off in one direction—this time east. I figured Antonia was doing as I suggested, heading for Texas.

We rode on at a steady pace till noon when we had to give the horses a blow, and I stood feeling weak and sore as hell and some of the drovers took out jerky from their saddlebags and chewed on it while we waited and others smoked. Waco was talking to one of his hands and looking over at me and I figured it could come at any moment—my execution. Then the two of them walked over and I could see now that he had his coat unbuttoned, Waco was heeled with a Colt revolver with staghorn grips riding his hip; he wore it butt forward in his holster.

"How'd you get involved in my business?" he said.

"Money," I said.

"You are going to live to regret your greed."

"I already do."

His gaze was unflinching. He removed his

Stetson and slapped it against his leg and I saw he had a receding hairline and was probably younger than he looked.

"Why carry me along on this?" I said.

He nodded as though I'd just told him something important and he was in agreement with me.

"I want you to see what I'm going to do to them—Antonia and your friend. I want you to watch them suffer before I kill you. You see, that's the way it is with me; I want to know that the man who crosses me does have to pay a heavy price. Shooting you in the head wouldn't give me any satisfaction. Having my men kill you slow after they've finished with her and him, that will give me satisfaction. You ever think you'd live to see a woman killed in a very bad way, Glass?"

I didn't doubt he'd do it and with his own hands. Me and Tom he might let his men do, but with Antonia he was going to extract his own personal revenge.

I could tell he was looking at the cuts and scratches on my face, examining them closely like a doctor might.

"You shouldn't have come into this county and gotten into my business," he said, then turned and walked away.

We were on the march again in thirty minutes. I couldn't help but wonder how Tom and

Antonia were going to outrun them riding double. I figured at best they had a couple hours lead on Waco, if that.

I figured by nightfall we'd all be dead.

CHAPTER TWENTY-EIGHT

The horse was starting to break down under their weight so they took turns walking, knowing it was going to slow them down.

At one point Tom said, "You go on."

"No," she said.

"They'll catch us at this rate. No point in both of us getting caught. Your husband doesn't know who I am. Even if they catch me, I can deny I even know you."

"You're the one with the broke arm," she said. "You best go on."

"I'm not the kind to leave a woman behind."

"Really? Don't tell me you're one of those do-gooders."

"How'd you know?"

She looked down at him and he was smiling.

They kept moving, neither one willing to give in. Late afternoon they reached a spring and knelt and drank using their hands to scoop up the cool clean water and filled the one canteen.

"You know where we're going?" he said.

"I think to Texas if we keep going this direction," she said.

"How far do you reckon it is to Texas?"

"It's a good ways yet."

Their horse drank. The sun was gaining strength. Things almost seemed normal.

"You think they're following us?" she said.

He shrugged. "You know him better than I do. I don't know him at all."

"I think they're following us."

"We better not sit here then."

"I think I recognize some of this country," she said.

He looked around.

"It all looks pretty much the same to me."

"I came up through here once with Johnny, back when things weren't so bad between us. He was going to a place called Gando to buy some horses. I don't think it's all that far from here."

"You think you can find it?"

"I think so."

They debated whose turn it was to ride; he finally convinced her it was hers.

By the time they topped a rock ridge and looked down on a set of shacks, the sun was a foot off the lip of the horizon.

"That's the place," she said. "That's Gando as I remember it."

He studied it.

"Looks deserted to me."

They each felt hope sink as they made their way down the loose rock slope.

He had been right, the place was deserted. The last of the day's light fell on ridged but rusty tin roofs that covered ill-constructed buildings of weathered gray planks, the broken glass of their windows glittering in the dying sun. A wind that cut down through a gorge whistled like a lonesome man as they stood there feeling defeated. The stock pens stood empty, as though they'd never been used. A couple of the buildings had been burnt to charred remnants.

They picked one of the buildings and tied off their horse and went inside knowing it wasn't much if any sort of refuge but knowing they couldn't go on either.

"I think this was the place where Johnny did business," she said, looking around. It was empty except for motes of dust swirling in the light. The floorboards creaked underfoot.

"What now?" she said.

"I was about to ask you the same thing."

"We can't go on, the horse is shot."

"I know it," he said.

"Wait here."

She left and returned carrying her saddlebags and set them on the floor between them then slid down and sat with her back against the wall, and he sat with his back against it too. She opened the bags and took out the two bottles—

one of wine and the other of whiskey and something else too: a small silver derringer.

"Whiskey and guns don't mix," he said, "so I've heard. What do you intend to do with that?"

She uncorked the bottle with the whiskey and took a long drink and said, "I don't know. But I figure when the time is right I'll know what to do with it." She held out the bottle for him. He declined.

"You *are* a do-gooder," she said.

"Why, because I won't drink with you?"

She looked suddenly sad. "I'm sorry. I guess I just think everyone should feel as miserable as I do."

He watched her tilt the bottle to her mouth again. "Tell me your story," he said.

She arched an eyebrow.

"I'd like to know more about you," he said. "I mean we have some time, right?"

"You tell me yours," she said.

So he began to tell her about himself and his late wife and how she died and his lonesome wanderings ever since and meeting Jim—how he'd found him and how it seemed to him all so strange and yet predestined somehow.

"Even this, the two of us sitting here waiting for death to come," he said, "seems to me somehow predetermined and I'm okay with that."

And after he finished she told him about herself, the pain of losing the person you loved and

285

being with someone you didn't, and somewhere in the middle of telling their stories, their hands met and held to each other and he even shared a little of the whiskey with her. And then they drank the wine. And by the time they'd done all this, the sun had set off in the west and the room had grown almost completely dark and he found an old bull's-eye lantern that still had some oil in it and lit it and sat back down next to her.

"When do you think they'll come?" she said.

"I don't know. It doesn't matter now, does it?"

"No, it doesn't."

"May I ask you something?"

She shrugged.

"I was wondering what it would be like to kiss you. Would you allow me to?"

She thought of Pedro, of his request to kiss her—how his voice and eyes spoke of the deep loneliness. His need wasn't born of desire. But Tom's was, and it raised her own desire as well.

"Funny," she said.

"What is?"

"I was just about to ask you the same thing, about kissing you."

"Because you're scared this may be the last time you ever kiss anyone?"

"No. I'm scared this may be the last time I ever get to feel something real again."

"That's what I was thinking too. But even if

those men weren't coming to kill us, I think I'd still want to kiss you."

She closed her eyes and tilted her face to him. He kissed her and she kissed him.

"Would you like to turn out the light?" she said as they held each other.

"Yes," he said.

CHAPTER TWENTY-NINE

As luck would have it—or fate, which he knew was how Tom would put it—the pursuit got delayed when the Indian's horse came up lame. There was some debate about what to do, and the sun was dropping out of the sky, making our shadows long.

"Why don't we just shoot that son of a bitch, boss, and give the Indian his horse," the man who seemed closest to Waco said.

"No, I'm saving him for something special. Let the Indian keep afoot."

So we went with that plan for a time and I was pretty amazed how much stamina the Indian had, running about as fast as a horse could trot, but even he couldn't keep it up long and stood at some point bent at the waist with his hands resting on his knees.

It had been a mistake on Waco's part to slow

the chase, and he realized it when the last light went out of the sky and we still hadn't caught up with Tom and Antonia. Waco cursed his decision and ordered his top hand to pick a man to give up his horse and stay behind come morning—that we'd make camp tonight. I was ordered away from the campfire and tied to the trunk of a small blackjack tree. I was also damn glad to be off a horse; every bounce rattled my already sore bones.

I sat there in the dark watching the others crowded around the campfire moving in and out of the light, filling their plates from a cook pot of beans and their cups with coffee. My belly crawled with hunger.

I tried closing my eyes and not thinking about what was going on or how hungry I was or how much I ached. It didn't do any good to think on it. Instead I thought about Maize and Fannie Watts and several of the other women I'd been with. Even if I hadn't loved them, they still provided me some nice memories—except for the bad parts—and I could lose myself thinking about them, about particular moments, and it helped ease my troubled self. About all a man has to rely on is his mind and what's in it and what all he's done in the past—the good and the bad. It's like looking through an album of photographs somebody took of your life and all the people you'd ever met.

I was roused from my reverie by the sound of approaching footsteps. A shadow stood over me when I looked up. He was holding something. I did not care.

"You remember me?" he said.

I shook my head.

"Bob," he said.

"Sorry, I don't."

He squatted down and I could see and then smell the plate of beans and the cup of coffee he was holding.

"You hungry?"

"This bound to be my last supper?" I said.

"No. I don't reckon it is," he said. "I think the boss wants to use you pretty good before he drops you down a hole." He leaned forward and untied me and then handed me the plate.

"Your boss know you're doing this?" I said.

He shrugged, said, "What do I give a shit?"

"Bob?" I said, trying to remember the name; nothing came to mind.

"Back at the line shack that day. Me and my pard came 'round and you jumped us and tied us up and I had to piss and you were decent enough not to make me piss in my drawers. You remember now?"

"Oh, yeah. I do."

"Go on and eat 'fore that gets cold."

I ate and he retied me to the tree.

"I figure this way we're even on things," he said.

289

"Much appreciated," I said.

He stood then. "Take care friend," he said.

"Wait."

He paused.

"We're not quite," I said.

"We're not quite what?"

"Even."

"How you figure? You done me a good turn and now I done you one."

"You remember the last thing I did that day?"

He stood silent.

"I left your ropes loose enough so you could work your way free."

"That make us even in your book, I was to do the same thing, knowing if Mr. Waco learned of it he'd probably break my hands then have the boys use me for target practice?"

"You seem like a man who don't let his debts go unpaid."

He looked back down to the campfire. A lot of the others were already wrapping up in their blankets for the night.

"Shit," he said, and bent and retied the ropes nice and loose.

I was already working my way out of them by the time I saw him dip into the camp's firelight. I stayed put until it looked like most everyone in the camp was asleep. The remuda was tied just on the other side of the campfire. I didn't have anything to lose.

I came up on the horses easy and untied the first one, a dark bay, and led him off away from the camp, rubbing his muzzle as we went. A gun or two would have been nice and so would a saddle, but all the guns and saddles were with those sleeping men and I couldn't risk charging into the camp.

Then something cold and hard pressed to the back of my skull and a low voice said, "Where do you think you're going?"

"Nowhere, I guess."

Then the pressure relieved itself and Bob stepped around in front of me and said, "You're probably going to need this," and handed me a Winchester.

"We're more than even now," I said.

"You goddamn straight we are."

I swung up on the back of the bay.

"Oh, by the way, that's Waco's horse. He's going to be real pissed you took it."

"What about you?" I said.

"Me? Shit, I'm in the wind as of this night. I guess I about used up any welcome I once had here."

I reached down a hand and he shook it and I heeled the horse to a walk moving away from the camp and didn't stop till I topped a ridge and looked back and it looked peaceful, the firelight flickering down there in the great darkness. I could see them rising in the morning, stretching and yawning and trying to work the kinks out of their stiff bones, because I'd done it a thousand times myself. I could see the man who came and told Waco his horse was stole and then hear the confusion about where old Bob had gone off to and how all I managed to get away.

The Indian would stand looking baleful as usual, not letting any of them read what was in his thoughts, and pretty quick they'd get it figured out and find Tom and Antonia and do their business.

I knew I had to reach them first.

CHAPTER THIRTY

He woke and wept alone—away from his wife, where she could not see or hear him. He held his broken hands up in the air and stared at them and it brought tears to his eyes each time he did. The bones had been more than broken, they had been smashed, and even though they were healing slowly, they would never heal right and he couldn't look into the future and imagine what it would be like to be a cripple after he had all his life made his living using his hands.

He worked his revolver out of its holster and tried to hold it and fumbled it and picked it up and tried again but it was a useless frustrating exercise. His fingers would not bend to the trigger, his thumb had no leveraging strength to cock the hammer. Even with two hands he had difficulty.

He had let everyone down—Antonia, his wife, and maybe the town, if Johnny Waco took it in his head to burn it down.

He hated having Nora see him this way. Hated having her wait on him, tie his shoes, button his shirt, while he held his broken hands like claws. He considered in those dark private moments of getting on a horse and just riding away. The townspeople looked on him with pity, kids stared at his hands. His two deputies showed no respect for him any longer. Life went on. He felt left behind.

On just such a morning there came a knock at the door and using both hands he fumbled the latch open and saw a face he hadn't seen in years.

"Chalk," the man said.

"Dalton."

The man was well-dressed in a fine suit and overcoat and a sugarloaf hat; he wore kidskin gloves. He was a tall angular man, well groomed with neatly waxed moustaches that were more gray than dark.

"You mind if I come in?"

Chalk stepped aside and the man entered, ducking his head slightly as he did.

"When'd you arrive in town?"

"Late last night, on the flyer," he said.

"Why you're here is the more important question."

"What happened to your hands, Chalk?"

He looked again at his hands then into the slate gray eyes of the visitor.

"Long story I'd just as soon not go into."

The man nodded and took off his hat as he followed Chalk into the front parlor—a small room just to the right of the front door whose windows looked out onto the street and were draped with tatted curtains.

Chalk nodded toward a chair with padded arms, and the man sat, crossed one leg over the other and rested his hat on his knee.

"I came to see my daughter," the man said.

"She's not here," Chalk replied.

"Perhaps you could tell me where she is?"

Chalk shrugged, said, "I ain't sure, Dalton."

"I see. I'd gotten a letter from her recently that concerned me. In it she wrote some veiled references. Antonia always was a bit cryptic. I thought I'd come and find out what's going on for myself."

"She's in trouble."

"Do you mind if I smoke?"

"No."

Dalton Stone took a ready made from a silver case and struck a match with his thumbnail and fired the end of the cheroot, then snapped out the match and looked for a place to set it. Chalk walked over to a small table and took a pewter tray from it with both hands and brought it to his visitor.

"Thank you."

There was a long moment of silence where only the sound of a clock in another room could be heard.

"Tell me about the trouble my daughter is in, Chalk."

"How much do you know about her?"

"Not much. It's been several years since I've seen her. She rarely writes. I knew she had left you when she thought you were dead and married John Waco, that he's a rancher. She didn't invite me to the wedding. I asked then if I could come and see her and meet him and she told me not to. I respected her wishes. I figured then there was a reason behind her not wanting me to meet her new husband and I am guessing the reason still holds true. That's why I came to you first."

"Johnny Waco turned out not to be a blessing to her."

"He's mistreated her?"

"I'm not sure how much or in what ways."

"Tell me what you do know."

"I know she left him and ended up here in Coffin Flats working for a man named Pink Huston."

"Odd name."

"Fits his profession."

"What do you mean?"

"Jesus, Dalton, I hate to even have to talk about this with you."

The man drew deeply on his cigarette and exhaled the smoke in a long blue stream, his gaze fixed on Chalk Bronson.

"Whatever it is, I can take it," he said.

"Pink runs a hog farm."

"You mean a house of prostitution."

"Yes."

"And Antonia became one of his girls?"

Chalk shrugged. "Something along those lines."

He saw Dalton stiffen but only slightly, saw him touch the brim of his hat resting upon his knee as though to brush something from it.

"So she's working for this Huston?"

"No, not anymore."

"Let's not be mysterious, Chalk. Say what you know."

Chalk told him the story—all of it that he knew so far. Dalton listened intently, stubbing out his cheroot by the time the marshal had finished.

"So you think this Jim Glass has gone to rescue her?"

Chalk looked at his hands.

"That was his intent, yes sir."

"But you don't think he's capable?"

"No sir. I don't see how with it being just him against Johnny Waco and all his men."

He saw Dalton Stone lower his gaze then in a contemplative manner, heard him take a deep breath and let it out again.

"Then I must go and do what I can," he said.

"I don't know what that would be, Mr. Stone."

"Nor do I."

"I'm sorry I let her down," Chalk said.

"Your hands," the man said. "Have you seen a doctor, and what does he say?"

"Says I'll be lucky to tie my own shoes once they heal."

Chalk watched as Dalton Stone took out a card and wrote something on it and handed it to him.

"That is the name and address of a doctor—a surgeon I know in Denver. I want you to go there and have him examine your hands. I'm sure there is something he can do for you."

"I appreciate it, but I can't afford trips to Denver and special doctors. I can't even get a job sweeping out a store . . ."

Dalton Stone took out a black leather wallet and took from it two hundred dollars and set it on the table next to the ashtray.

"For tickets and a place to stay. Tell Dr. Jameson to send me his bill."

"I can't accept your charity."

"The hell you can't. Don't be a fool. You were always good to my daughter as far as I know and you tried to help her when she was in trouble and it's little enough I help you now."

Chalk felt contrite, slightly embarrassed, but grateful.

"I'd like to hire as many men as I can—men who aren't afraid to use a gun. Can you recommend any?"

"Not in this county, but the next county over maybe. I've got a contact or two there."

"Can you send a telegram on my behalf to your contact?"

"Yeah, I can."

"How long do you think before your man could get some people here?"

"Two days."

"No sooner?"

"Two days would probably be the soonest."

"Then if you would."

"Yes sir."

"I'll be at the hotel, just ask for me."

"Yes sir."

Dalton put a hand on Chalk's shoulder. "I'm sorry about your hands."

"I would have let him cut them off if it would have saved her."

"I believe that you would, Chalk."

He put the sugarloaf hat back on his head and went out, and when Chalk turned back from the door, his wife was standing there.

"Who was that?" she said. "And would you

really have traded your hands for her?"

He didn't know how to tell her—how a man could love two women at the same time, how he could give his hands or even his very life for either one. There were just some things you couldn't explain.

CHAPTER THIRTY-ONE

I knew I'd never be able to locate Tom and Antonia in the dark, and even when it grew light I'd have a hell of a time finding them. So instead of riding away trying to stay ahead of Waco's men I went up to a ridge and waited. It was a long cold night of waiting and two or three times I started awake from a doze.

But finally the dawn came over a ridgeline or rocks to the east and I saw the small figures in the distant camp below me stirring awake. I saw too the small panic among them when they found out I was missing. It seemed to quicken their pace and in short order they were riding out, led by the Indian, except two left short of horses.

I kept my distance in following them. If the Indian was as good today as he had been yesterday he'd find my friends for me.

We rode till near noon and then I saw them stop atop a bluff of red sandstone. I wasn't quite able to see what they were looking at below. But it looked like Waco gave them orders and they descended the bluff slowly.

By the time I reached the spot where they had been I saw what they'd been looking at: a collection of shacks, a ghost town, it seemed.

Waco's men were spreading out through it then they gathered around one building in particular that had a weary looking horse tied up in front.

I could hear them shouting something.

Then suddenly there were two shots spaced out about a second apart followed by utter and stunned silence. I had dismounted and lay flat on the sandstone with my rifle ready. I had it aimed at the fellow wearing the sheepskin coat.

Several of the men dismounted down below and cautiously approached the building, their pistols drawn. Johnny Waco sat his horse, content, I suppose, to let his boys do the dirty work.

Like rats, the men slipped in through the doors and windows.

I held my breath, keeping the front blade of the Winchester aimed at the center of Johnny Waco's back.

And when the men came out dragging the bodies of Tom and Antonia and laid them at the feet of Johnny's horse, I pulled the trigger and watched him topple from the saddle and fall beside them.

It set up panic among them of course, and I shot

the Indian next just because he was the son of a bitch that led them to my friends. And then I shot another and another until I had shot at least half a dozen before they figured where the firing was coming from and had scattered like quail into the buildings.

But I was already riding back down the ridge, circling in a wide loop, maybe one or two shells left in my rifle, my mind full of anger. I figured if they were fool enough to come after me, I'd take them away from the ghost town and circle back and get more weapons and make my stand. And if it came to dying with my friends, then I figured it was a hell of a lot better than dying without them.

I reached a point far enough away to wait to see if they were coming. I waited listening for the sounds of pounding hooves.

Nobody came.

I waited some more.

Still, nobody came.

I completed my loop and came within sight of the ghost town from the northwest. The bodies were all still there, lying like rag dolls, but the drovers were gone. I saw a dust cloud the other side of the valley. I figured it was Waco's boys, fled, all the fight taken out of them now that the man paying their wages wouldn't be anymore. Besides, if they were any sort of drovers, it would have been damn demeaning taking orders from a dead son of a bitch. Drovers, if nothing else, are pretty goddamn independent even if someone's paying them regular wages.

I waited a bit longer to make sure some of those old boys didn't come back out of a sense of misguided loyalty, then rode on down.

Tom and Antonia lay side by side as if they'd simply fallen asleep. She was yet beautiful even in death, and Tom looked as peaceful as he had ever been. I noticed how their hands touched. Each had a small bloody wound to the side of the head but were otherwise unmarked.

Johnny lay facedown next to them, his face in the dirt turned away from the woman he'd wanted to possess more than he'd wanted to love.

My curiosity caused me to go inside the building I'd seen Waco's men drag them from. I found a small silver derringer with both shells spent and it confirmed my suspicions. Tom had done for her what she could not have done for herself. And knowing him, he probably told her he wouldn't let her go alone into that dark void, that he'd go with her just to keep her company.

I walked out again feeling sad and bitter because it shouldn't have turned out this way.

I scoured the ruined little town until I found the busted blade of a shovel with half a handle someone had left behind, as if whoever had left it knew it still had a purpose.

I dug a single grave and put Tom and Antonia

in it, side by side. I suspected they would have wanted it that way—that she would have wanted him to hold her and that he would have wanted to hold her on their final journey.

My hands shook as I tossed the last shovel of dirt onto the mound and patted it down. I told myself that my tears were from anger and not from sorrow, but they were from both and I didn't really care.

Then I rode away again, as I had once come, a stranger to this place, these dead.

EPILOGUE

As they waited for the end they spoke of many things and told each other things about themselves they'd not told anyone until that time.

They slept and woke again and talked more and she told him of all the things she'd hoped she would have become if life had turned out differently, and all the places she would have liked to have traveled. And he told her of similar dreams he had, saying he had lost his way but understood there was reason to be found even in the confusion of being lost.

"One life is not enough," he said. "We should have three or four. One in which we learn, and another in which we live what we've learned, and one we spend in pleasure and one in which we spend in reflection."

"How do you know that we don't?" she said. "How do you know that when we die we don't go on to another life and do exactly that, and that maybe this is the life of reflection we are living now and all the other lives await us still?"

"I don't know," he said.

"Do you believe there are other lives after this one?"

"Yes, I do," he said.

"So do I."

"Then it won't be so bad, will it?"

"No. I don't think it will be very bad at all."

"It might be so beautiful we can't even begin to imagine it," he said.

"I'd like to believe that."

"Then we should."

"Yes."

And then they fell into silence, each feeling their separate thoughts as they held hands until she leaned against him and said, "Hold me, Tom."

And so he held her in his embrace knowing what was to come.

For they'd decided somewhere between that long night and when they heard the riders come that they would suffer no more at the hands of others.

She handed him the derringer.

"I want to go first," she said.

He nodded.

They heard the horses stop outside.

"It's time," she said. "Before they come in."

"Yes," he said. "Let me kiss you one last time."

She inclined her head to him and he kissed her.

Then they heard footsteps on the porch outside. She closed her eyes. He pulled the trigger once. Then he said, "Good-bye my sweet, sweet child," and pulled the trigger again.

Twenty men arrived from the adjoining county and Chalk was waiting for them.

"You boys go over to the Bison and get you something to eat and something to drink and I'll go and get Mr. Stone and he'll tell you what he needs and what the pay is," he said, and they went quietly knowing that work was work and sometimes hard to come by unless you were willing to do whatever it was needed doing and were not afraid.

And just as he came out of the hotel with Mr. Stone walking at his side he saw the stranger riding down the street on a lathered horse.

The stranger stopped, and Chalk said to Mr. Stone, "This is Jim Glass. Jim, this is Mr. Dalton Stone, Antonia's father."

And the two men shook hands and then Jim told him about the daughter he had come to find and where he could find her.

"Would you be kind enough to show me?" Mr. Stone said.

"I would."

And together they rode back out to the ghost town and Jim showed the father where the daughter was buried and explained to him the story and circumstance of her death and about his friend Tom Twist and what sort of man he was.

"I know he did right by her," Jim said. "I don't

doubt that by the end he had come to love her."
And after Dalton Stone had knelt there by her
grave for a time, he stood and looked around
and said, "You killed these men?"

"I did."

"Which one is Johnny Waco?"

Jim showed him.

"And would you, sir, do such a thing again if
the need called for it?"

"I would," said Jim.

"Then we need to talk, you and I."

And together they rode back to Coffin Flats,
two men who were once strangers but now had
found a common cause.

Center Point Publishing

600 Brooks Road ● PO Box 1
Thorndike ME 04986-0001 USA

(207) 568-3717

US & Canada:
1 800 929-9108
www.centerpointlargeprint.com